The kiss caught Betsy off balance as well as off guard.

She was falling, metaphorically, she thought, into the deep and aching sweetness of the kiss, until her shoulder collided roughly with something solid and warm and the smoky fragrance of dying leaves burst in her nostrils.

The impact dragged her mouth free of Charles's, and opened her eyes. They had fallen—at least the duke had—in a lush windsweep of jewel-toned leaves beneath the oak tree holding his kite captive. His shoulder had cushioned her fall, and she lay, Betsy realized with a shocked gasp, almost completely on top of him, still locked in his embrace. . . .

Also by Jane Lynson
Published by Fawcett Books:

CAPTAIN RAKEHILL

THE DUKE'S DOWNFALL

Jane Lynson

FAWCETT CREST • NEW YORK

A Fawcett Crest Book
Published by Ballantine Books
Copyright © 1992 by Lynn Smith

Library of Congress Catalog Card Number: 91-93149

ISBN 0-449-21725-6

Manufactured in the United States of America

First Edition: April 1992

For Aunt Jane

Chapter One

When the Dowager Countess of Clymore's letter reached her house in Berkeley Square, the butler, Iddings, gathered his staff in the servants' hall and read, in sepulchral tones, the brief missive announcing the planned arrival of her ladyship and her granddaughter, Lady Elizabeth Keaton, in town the Tuesday next. The news caused several of the housemaids to swoon, and three of the footmen to give immediate notice.

The hartshorn was sent for, the resignations filled with brawny types more the like of sailors than footmen, and preparations for her ladyship's arrival began. Each and every saloon was swept of anything breakable (hence the classically uncluttered look so remarked upon by the countess's set), the heaviest pieces of furniture were repositioned at the corners of the carpets, and the more fragile chairs and settees removed to the attics.

It was, when added to the usual scrubbing, airing, dusting, beating, and polishing, a colossal undertaking. The pipe clay put down on the freshly washed front steps to whiten them had scarce had a chance to dry when the bedlamite clamor heralding the approach of the countess's carriage was heard outside the spiked iron fence enclosing the house.

Shouting at two of the strapping, newly hired footmen to man the gates, Iddings kept the third at his side and took up his place on the doorstep. When a deep crimson landau careened into the courtyard on wheels thick with road dust, Iddings signed to the footmen, and the gates swung shut on the pack of dogs, urchins, and cats yelping and yowling along in the wake of the carriage.

In the box, next to the portly driver possessed of nerves of steel, perched a greatcoat-swathed figure in charge of the leads and the horses thundering the landau toward the house. On the crimson leather squabs sat the dowager, clearly nonplussed by the alarming cant at which the landau was negotiating the curved yard.

The ends of the emerald ribbons securing her ladyship's chipstraw bonnet to her head fluttered beneath her ears, while beside her loomed a creature so large that it could, but for its shaggy coat and the deep, excited rumbling issuing from its throat, be mistaken for a fifth to the perfectly matched grays all but sitting back on their tails to slow the carriage and bring it to a halt.

"Beggin' yer pardon, sir," muttered the footman to Iddings, "but what manner of beast *is* that?"

" 'Tis a dog, you dolt," the butler replied disdainfully. "An Irish hound."

As the landau rolled to a stop before the steps, the coachman fished from his waistcoat pocket a watch on a gold fob, a gift from the dowager on his twenty years' service to the Keatons of Clymore. He peered at the gilt face, then grinned at his companion.

2

"Smartly done, Lady Betsy. Shaved seven minutes whole off yer best time."

"That's ten pounds then, if you please, Granmama." Lady Elizabeth Keaton tugged off the oversized, flop-eared hat pulled low over her brow to conceal her blond curls and turned on the high seat to hold out a leather-gloved hand. "You wagered I could trim no more than five."

As she turned, the heavy, caped coat fell from her shoulders to reveal her slim figure and rumpled blue velvet traveling costume. Despite the wrinkles, her drooping coiffure, and the road dust smudging her nose, Lady Elizabeth had blossomed from the thin, awkward girl Iddings had last seen four years ago into a delectably lovely young lady.

Her lengthy stay at Clymore—enforced by the death of her father following a hunting accident and lengthy illness—had, despite the circumstances, done her obvious good. If the countess could keep check on her granddaughter's impulsiveness, a trait borne in the Keaton blood, she would, Iddings thought, have no trouble firing the girl off.

"Ten pounds and worth every penny," the dowager replied sternly, "so long as you keep to your promise that there will be no more driving, no more wagering, and no more conversing with young gentlemen in Greek simply to make them look cloth-headed."

"I do so swear, Granmama," Betsy vowed solemnly.

"Then 'tis a bargain well made." As her ladyship removed the gloved hand she'd wrapped around the hound's thick collar in order to open her reticule, he leaped from the landau and shot across the

3

courtyard toward the mob of strays still milling outside the wrought-iron fence.

"Boru!" the countess screeched. "Come back here!"

More sensibly, Iddings shouted, "Stop him!"

Understanding now precisely why they'd been hired, the two footmen at the gate rushed the giant hound gamboling toward them. In the box, Lady Elizabeth plucked the glove from her right hand, stuck two fingers in the corners of her mouth, and gave a short, piercing whistle. Boru wheeled and trotted back to the landau, leaving the footmen to skid to a disgruntled halt and watch the hound, tail swishing the cobbles, sit obediently down on his haunches before the landau. The dowager eyed him balefully; his mistress adoringly as she swung herself down from the box.

"You are too bad, Boru," Betsy chided fondly, taking the hound's huge, opened jaws between her hands and rubbing her nose against his.

Boru whined and swathed his long pink tongue across her face. Lady Clymore clapped her hands disapprovingly.

"Stand straight, gel!" she shrilled. "And no more whistling like a cowherd!"

"How else was I to stop him?" Betsy inquired as she straightened. "Please trust, Granmama," she went on, with a wave about the courtyard, "that I have sense enough to whistle only within privacy of our own property."

"Kindly make certain you do not forget."

"Of course I will not," Betsy replied, and lowered her gaze.

But not before Iddings glimpsed the gleam in her violet-blue eyes. It was devilment, of that he was certain, for that same impish twinkle had been in her eyes the day he'd caught her sprinkling salt instead of sugar on a plateful of biscuits laid out for her grandmother's tea.

"The steps," he hissed, elbowing the new man.

Gingerly edging past the girl and the huge dog, the footman placed the steps and opened the carriage door. The slightly stooped but still spry countess alighted, her sharp eyes assessing the breadth of the man's shoulders.

"You're new, aren't you? What's your name?"

"George, m'lady," the man replied, with a bow.

"Well then, George, I should like you to meet Brian Boru," she said, nodding grimly at the hound. "The apple of my granddaughter's eye, and the bane of my existence."

Boru hung his head and whimpered.

"Granmama." Betsy *tsk*ed and laid a soothing hand between the dog's shaggy ears. "You've hurt his feelings."

"I should like to hurt more than that," her ladyship muttered, then fixed a commanding eye on the footman. "Since you are of a particular size, George, and Boru requires a firm hand, I am entrusting him to your care."

"He is gentle as a lamb," Betsy countered, "and *I* have always seen to Boru."

"You will be far too busy," her grandmother informed her crisply, and turned again to George. "He requires exercise thrice daily. I suggest the back garden, where the wall is quite high. He eats at nuncheon and supper, and feeds like Prinny. Inform Cook to henceforth consider the Regent himself in residence." From the depths of her voluminous reticule, the countess withdrew a consid-

5

erable length of stout leather strap and placed it in the footman's hands. "I think Boru should like a run now, George."

"Y-yes, m'lady." The footman swallowed hard and turned to face his charge.

At sight of his lead, Boru lifted his ears and began to quiver with anticipation. He stretched his great head eagerly toward George and gave a single, deep-throated *woof* that caused his new keeper to nearly leap out of his livery.

"He is quite tame," Betsy assured him, torn between pity for the poor fellow and fury at her grandmother for painting such a monstrous picture of her darling. She took the lead from George, knelt, and fastened it to Boru's collar. "He is very strong, but very gentle. He will be a bit frisky from the journey, but will give you no trouble." Betsy offered the looped end of the strap with an encouraging smile. "So long as you hold on tight."

The footman swallowed again. "I'll do that, m'lady."

No sooner had his fingers closed on the lead than Boru was off, jerking the unfortunate George off his feet. Toes scarcely touching the ground, he bounced along in Boru's wake like a dinghy on rough seas.

"Why couldn't you have been content with a Pekinese?" Lady Clymore demanded of her granddaughter, as hound and footman disappeared around the corner of the house.

"Boru is my only friend in the world," Betsy stated, not bitterly but matter-of-factly, "and my last gift from Papa. I'll not allow you to separate me from him, Granmama."

"If you've naught but a hound to befriend you," Lady Clymore retorted, " 'tis but your own fault.

Your antics have quite put off any young ladies who would associate with you, and no gentleman will offer for a girl who can outride and outthink him."

"A peahen could accomplish the latter," Betsy shot back. "And I should like to point out that you were a far better markswoman than I, a top-of-the-trees sawyer, and that you once nicked Grandfather—Lord rest his soul—for fifty pounds at Hazard. The very accomplishments I learned from you—nay, that you took such pains to *teach* me—you now refer to me as *my* antics!"

" 'Twas a different world when I was a girl," her ladyship declared vehemently. "What then was considered admirable and sauce for the goose, is now thought shocking and no more than scandal broth for the gosling! You must keep to your promise if you truly wish to find yourself a husband. If you do not, we may as well turn the carriage about this instant and return to Clymore!"

"Where dear Julian waits to snatch me up as he snatched up Papa's title?" Betsy taunted, her voice tinged with bitterness. "I warn you, Granmama, I will *never* marry that toad-eating cousin of mine!"

"That toad-eater," her grandmother replied between clenched teeth, "though it pains me to even think it, is the Earl of Clymore now."

"You loathe him as much as I, yet you would see me shackled to him!"

"He is head of the family, you silly gel! You should be on your knees with gratitude that I managed to persuade him to give you until Christmas to make a match of your own!"

"With the clear understanding," Betsy retorted, "that if I do *not*, I will marry *him*! I cannot credit, Granmama, that you have taken the word of a penniless mushroom as that of a gentleman! He has no intention of allowing me to marry elsewhere! Not when he so desperately needs my inheritance to support himself in style as the Earl of Clymore!"

"Neither of us has a choice in the matter," Lady Clymore replied bluntly. "It is the way of the world. You must marry someone else or accept Julian!"

"I'd sooner take the devil than Julian Dameron!" Betsy lifted her skirts and dashed up the stairs. On the top step she spun about to deliver a last scathing remark, and from her vantage next to Iddings saw the footmen shooing the ragged band of children and dogs away from the fence. "Wait!" Betsy quickly descended the steps. "Silas," she said to the coachman, "my reticule, please."

He handed it down to her from the box, and Betsy opened it to remove her coin purse as she crossed the courtyard.

"You'll only encourage them to hang about when they should be working!" her grandmother called after her.

But for a subtle squaring of her shoulders and purposeful stiffening of her stride, Betsy ignored her. Throwing up her hands in disgust, the dowager marched up the stairs.

"Welcome, my lady," Iddings said, and bowed.

"And what do you think of that?" Hesper Keaton demanded of her majordomo. "Giving her pin money to urchins?"

"I think," Iddings replied, "that she has as kind and generous a heart as you, my lady."

"Hmph." The countess sniffed disparagingly, but her cheeks pinked. "I'll greet the staff now, Iddings. Any changes beyond George and the two at the gates?"

"None, my lady." He nodded to a junior footman and escorted her to the chair placed for her in the foyer.

While the man hurried away to summon the staff from the servants' hall, Iddings moved to close the doors. As he paused in the threshold to watch Lady Elizabeth dispense coins to the children through the bars of the fence, the coachman caught his eye and winked. Iddings returned the wink, then quietly shut the doors as Silas swung down from the box to light his pipe and keep a watchful eye on Betsy.

The last coin in her purse was a half crown, and the last child was a boy with brown hair, hanging back from the gates clutching a string fastened to the neck of a scruffy dog that looked to be mostly terrier. Both were alarmingly thin and filthy. Betsy's heart went out to him as she slipped her hand through the bars and offered the coin on her gloved palm.

"Go on," she said gently. "Take it."

The child's eyes widened at the half crown, then shuttered warily. "What fer?"

"For helping me win my wager with my grandmother."

" 'Ow'd I 'elp?"

"By making my horses run even faster." Betsy stretched her hand a little farther and smiled. "You've earned it, along with my thanks."

A prideful grin lit the boy's dirty face and he accepted the coin, lifting it from Betsy's palm and tucking it in the folds of the rags he wore for clothes.

"S'all right, miss. Right fun it wuz."

"Yes, it was right fun. Thank you again."

The boy nodded, tugged on the dog's string to

turn away, but wheeled abruptly back to look at Betsy. "You be goin' out again soon, miss?"

"On the morrow," she replied, with a smile. "I've some shopping to do."

"So do me an' Scraps." He grinned again, flashed the coin from the depths of his rags, then darted away down the square with his little dog limping on three legs behind him.

Chapter Two

*W*hen Betsy and her grandmother left Berkeley Square the next day in a smart yellow phaeton with shiny black wheels, Boru was between them on the leather squabs and Silas at the ribbons. Neither the dowager or her granddaughter saw the brown-haired boy and his scruffy dog leap up from the curbside to scurry along in their wake, but Boru did.

With an excited whine, he lifted his ears and turned his head. Betsy shifted on the banquette to see what had caught his attention and glimpsed the boy and Scraps nipping and darting through the crowds on the flagway to keep pace with the phaeton.

The little terrier was still hopping on three legs, which caused Betsy to frown until she saw the happy wagging of his tail and the jaunty salute tossed her by the boy. She smiled then, raised her hand to wave at him, and received a sound rap on the wrist with the dowager's fan.

"Ouch!" Betsy shook her hand and glared at her grandmother.

"A polite nod," Lady Clymore scolded as she leaned around Boru, "is sufficient to acknowledge an acquaintance on the street."

11

"Yes, Granmama." Betsy sighed with feigned resignation, settled back on the squabs, and gave Boru an unseen pat of gratitude.

Already her plan was working. Quite satisfactorily, she thought, as she admired the welt swelling on her stinging wrist. She'd expected a battle when she'd suggested bringing Boru, but her grandmother had surprised her by agreeing.

"Capital idea," she'd approved. "With all the rabble flocking to town since the end of the war, he'll serve as an excellent deterrent to cut purses."

"But, Granmama," Betsy had reminded her innocently, "Boru won't bite his own fleas."

"*You* know that and so do I," the dowager had replied, with a cat-in-the-cream smile, "but the footpads do not."

Falling victim to a cut purse was probably too much to hope for, but Betsy, her reticule stuffed to bursting with an odd assortment of items smuggled to town in her hatboxes, was prepared for any contingency. Her father's pistol, its firing pin safely removed, would create a suitable sensation on the off-chance they should happen to be waylaid. And if Fate failed to throw a thief in her path, she was equally well armed with her grandfather's reading spectacles or his jeweled snuffbox, either one of which could be whipped out for suitable effect at a moment's notice.

Only as a last resort did Betsy plan to be shocking, for she had no wish to disgrace herself or her grandmother. Outrageous, yes, shocking only if it became absolutely necessary, but she did not think it would be to turn Julian Dameron's mercenary affections. Her intent was merely to avoid marriage—to her upstart cousin or anyone else—until her heart decreed otherwise.

There were heiresses aplenty to fill Julian's pockets with blunt, and all Betsy had to do to convince him she was a poor choice was behave like a Keaton. An easy task, since she had a lifetime of practice. His overweening pride and scrupulous desire to always be and do the proper thing would see to the rest. Betsy was sure of it—just as certain as she was that despite his agreement with her grandmother, Julian had every intention of following them to town to protect his interest in her considerable portion.

Ergo, Betsy was ready. With her reticule full of oddments and Boru beside her, she was invincible. Whatever remote possibility she may have overlooked in her planning, ever lovable and overzealous Boru could be counted on to deal with in the most unexpected and outlandish fashion imaginable, for he, too, had a lifetime of practice.

Looping her arm around his neck, Betsy smiled and settled back on the banquette to enjoy the city sights. When she wasn't glancing over her shoulders to see if the boy and Scraps were still following, she studied the occupants of the carriages they passed, particularly the ladies and the cut and style of their gowns. Their first stop was the modiste, and Betsy wished to be seen in the highest kick of fashion. It would make the part she intended to play seem even more incongruous.

When Silas reined the grays to avoid a near collision just ahead, she was deeply engrossed in the deftly tucked bodice of a blue merino walking dress making its way along the flagway on a plump young matron. If her arm hadn't been draped around Boru, she would've been pitched headlong onto the floor by the sudden stop. The jolt snapped her head up sharply, just as it did to the gentleman occupying the carriage drawing to an equally abrupt halt beside the phaeton.

As he lifted his head from whatever held his attention below the level of the window, Betsy caught her breath at the glimpse she had of his handsome profile. His very dark hair was wind-tossed, due to the breeze billowing through the lowered window and the fact that he was hatless. Odd as it was to see a gentleman sans chapeau, it was even more astounding to see one raise a book to carefully mark his place before closing it.

A very *thick* book, Betsy noted, all but gasping with astonishment. Intrigued, she watched him lean toward the window and peer about as if looking for someone, the cool sunshine streaking his wind-blown hair with blue highlights.

His eyes were blue—no, green—and he was clearly looking about for something. Or someone, Betsy thought, just as his gaze lifted and locked with hers. His eyes were neither blue nor green, but a mix of the two. And they were, she thought, the most intelligent eyes she'd ever seen.

If he felt at all taken aback by finding himself nearly nose-to-nose with her, it did not show in his expression. He did blink, but only as he turned his head to take quick, keen stock of their carriages stopped side by side in the midst of Oxford Street. When he looked back at her, the corners of his eyes had lifted, along with those of his mouth, in a smile of bemused surprise.

"Good day, my lady," he said, unlatching the carriage door and swinging it open to jump down. His deep voice was pleasant and matter-of-fact, as if meeting in the middle of a busy London street were as common as dust.

"Good day, sir," Betsy replied, matching his calm tone despite the quiver of excitement his smile sent racing up her spine.

Beside her, Boru whined and began to tremble. She laid a hand on his shoulder to soothe him, but he only whined again and gave a short, throaty bark that caused both teams to flatten their ears and back in their traces. It also alerted the coachman to the untoward creak of the springs, and turned him in his box to call urgently to his passenger, "No, no, Yer Grace! We're no where's near Piccadilly!"

"Your Grace!" Betsy breathed, her eyes widening. Why, he's a duke, she thought amazedly, quite the nicest—and the youngest—she'd ever met.

"Yes, Fletcher, I'm *aware* of that," he replied, patient reassurance in his voice as he looked up at his driver.

"Betsy! How many times must I tell you—" The dowager leaned around Boru and froze in midscold as she beheld the duke's face. "Good heavens, Braxton! You are half in and half out of your carriage!"

"Yes, Lady Clymore, I am." He stiffened then, as if suddenly remembering something, and shifted his gaze to address the dowager countess. His eyes, which only moments before had sparkled with humor and quick intelligence, now looked vacant and clouded with bewilderment. "I am?" he repeated, making a question of it. "I mean, I *am*, Lady Clymore. But you see, I thought this was Piccadilly."

"Yes, of course," her ladyship replied, with an

ironically arched brow. "Soho is so often mistaken for it."

Only by a complete dolt, thought Betsy, which the Duke of Braxton was not. The unanswerable question was why on earth he was trying to pass himself off as one.

His blacks chose that moment to chafe at the delay by rearing in their traces, which sent the carriage rocking, the duke weaving precariously to-and-fro, and Boru springing up on all fours. Vexed by the blacks and the hound's barking, Betsy's grays tried to bolt. The phaeton lurched forward before Silas could regain control, and Boru, before Betsy could restrain him, launched himself at the carriage.

The dowager valiantly flung herself across the banquette to catch him, but succeeded only in bumping so hard into Betsy that she sent her granddaughter tumbling to the floor. Only when both conveyances had stopped pitching and both teams had been calmed, did Betsy dare pick herself up to see what had happened. She had to sweep Boru's tail aside to look, and when she did, she cringed and groaned.

Pinned against the squabs by Boru, who was stretched between the phaeton and the duke's carriage, the countess turned her head as best she could against his shaggy flank and glared at Betsy.

"Get this oaf off me," she said between clenched teeth.

"This instant, Granmama." Betsy bolted from the phaeton, calling to Silas as she rounded the boot, "Hold them steady!"

George jumped down from the box and met her beside Boru. The crowd that had gathered to watch the argument between the two drivers who'd nearly collided but had settled the matter and moved on, now drifted down the flagway to gape and twitter at the huge dog strung between the two vehicles. Boru, clinging to the carriage window by his toenails, turned his head toward Betsy and whined imploringly.

"I'll have him down in a wink, m'lady." George raised his arms over his head, gripped Boru's front legs, and glanced at the duke's coachman. "Pull away real slow, guv."

The man nodded and did so. As the carriage inched forward, George lowered Boru's front paws onto his shoulders. The veins in his neck bulged with the effort of supporting the hound's weight, but slowly he managed to back Boru into the phaeton. Once all four of his feet were firmly planted on the banquette, Boru leaped into the countess's lap, leaned over the side, and licked George's face.

Her grandmother shrieked furiously, the crowd cheered, and Betsy raced toward the Duke of Braxton's carriage. The coachman had set the brake and climbed down to place the steps when Betsy reached the door, flung it open, and saw the duke sprawled inelegantly on the floor of the coach.

The sight of him made her heart lurch. Her plan was working, all right, far too well. This was no mere baronet spread-eagled and semiconscious before her, this was a *duke*! This was not outrageous, this was disastrous. Thinking only of her grandmother's wrath if she saw him, Betsy impulsively reached into the carriage, clutched the duke's forest green left sleeve in both hands, and pulled.

"Up, Your Grace!" she urged, tugging and puffing at his weight. "Quickly—up!"

With a groggy shake of his head, he tried to push himself up on his right arm. Encouraged, Betsy dug the heels of her soft kid half boots into the paving stones, leaned back to give herself more leverage, and nearly fell backward in a heap when the shoulder seam of his coat gave way with a loud *r-i-i-p*.

Horrified, Betsy clapped her gloved hands over her mouth as the duke sat up abruptly, shook his head to clear it, and raised his left arm. The cuff of his sleeve drooped off his fingertips and the snowy white lawn of his shirt gaped through the tear in his shoulder. He gazed at it a moment, nonplussed, then raised his eyes to Betsy's face.

"Was I not quick enough?"

"Oh *no*, Your Grace! The stitches simply gave way! I'm so dreadfully *sorry*! But I'm sure it can be repaired. Why, a clever seamstress—" clasping the hem of his wilted cuff, Betsy tugged the sleeve back into place to show him—"with a stitch here, a stitch there—"

Her overstuffed and very heavy reticule, sent swinging like a pendulum from her left elbow, at that moment reached the farthest point of its arc— which just happened to coincide with the space occupied by the Duke of Braxton's face. He caught the blow squarely on his jaw, with a solid clunk that sent him reeling backward.

"Your Grace!" Betsy shrieked, appalled. "Pray, are you hurt? I'm so *very* sorry! Oh, please, let me help you!"

As she reached out to take hold of him again, the duke scrambled quickly backward and away from her.

"There's no need," he said, lifting his sagging sleeve to rub his jaw. "I thank you for your concern, but I'm all right. Please feel free, young lady, to rejoin Lady Clymore and get the devil—er—continue on your way."

Young lady! Betsy's cheeks scalded and her temper flared. He was addressing her as if she were a child. "I am a lady, Your Grace, but not an especially young one, for I shall be one and twenty on my next birthday."

The duke arched one brow as Betsy, too late, bit her tongue on the faux pas. To tell him her age, she might as well have told him the color of her petticoat. But having said it, she had no choice but to brazen it out, and so went on haughtily, "I own it is my stature—or lack of it—which is deceptive. Though I am quite mature, I am often taken to be much younger."

"Perhaps it is your demeanor rather than your stature that causes the confusion," he suggested. "It would appear that you and your pet are well suited. Is he often mistaken for a horse?"

"Only," Betsy retorted, stung by his setdown, "by the very ignorant or the very shortsighted."

"Young lady," the duke replied flatly, "I am not so lacking in wit or vision that I cannot recognize a menace to public safety. In future, kindly curb your pet. With a sharp bit and leathers if necessary."

"I am *not* a young lady, and Boru is *not* a menace! But you, sirrah, are a—"

"That is *quite* enough, Betsy." Lady Clymore appeared at her side, her hastily righted bonnet perched atop her frayed hair like a hen on a haystack. "Before you cut up too stiff, allow me to present you to the Duke of Braxton. Charles Earnshaw, my granddaughter, Elizabeth Keaton."

"Your Grace," Betsy said, with the barest hint of a curtsey.

"Your servant," he replied coolly.

"What have you done to your coat?" the dowager asked.

"My coat?" The duke took his hand away from his jaw and peered at his sleeve. "Apparently, Lady Clymore, I've torn it." The tone of his voice suggested he'd just noticed.

Which was, Betsy knew, as false as his befuddled frown. The flush staining her cheeks was genuine, however, and she ducked her chin to hide it. Toplofty the Duke of Braxton might be, yet he was also uncommonly kind to keep to himself the particulars of how his coat came to be torn.

"Come to town for the Little Season, are you?" the dowager inquired.

"No," replied the duke, "for my brother Lesley's wedding. And to consult with an acquaintance of mine at the British Museum on a matter of historical significance. Unfortunately he's in Paris just now, examining Boney's plunder on behalf of His Highness."

"With any luck," the countess remarked dryly, "your acquaintance will find something Prinny can readily turn into blunt."

"Let us pray," the duke agreed, a smile easing his tight jaw, which was already showing a faint bruise.

Leaning back on his hands with his torn sleeve, rumpled waistcoat, and mussed hair, he looked more boyish than before, which only served to make Betsy feel guiltier—and fire her curiosity. One moment Charles Earnshaw seemed as high in the instep as any duke in the realm, the next a complete chuckle-head. It simply did not fadge.

"I trust my granddaughter has made apologies for Boru," the dowager said, giving Betsy a warning pinch on the elbow. "Horrid creature, but she's quite devoted to him. I trust you are unhurt?"

"I seem to be, yes."

"Then please give my regards to your mother." Her ladyship smiled and closed a firm hand on Betsy's arm. "And tell her I shall call upon her soon."

"She'll be delighted."

"Then good day to you, Braxton."

"Good day, Lady Clymore." The duke's gaze flicked ever so briefly over Betsy. "And to you, young lady."

Despite the gallantry he'd shown her, Betsy felt a purely childish impulse to stick her tongue out at him. And she might have, if her grandmother hadn't jerked her arm and marched her back to the phaeton, where George waited to assist them, and Boru, securely lashed to the far door by his lead, sat head down and shamefaced on the banquette.

"Granmama, how could you!"

"Keep your voice down or you will be tied and gagged beside him!" The dowager gave Betsy a none-too-gentle push into George's hands.

The footman gave her an apologetic smile as he handed her up into the phaeton. Smiling back forgivingly, she plunked unhappily down beside Boru and looped a consoling arm about his neck.

The excitement done with, the crowd on the flagway began to mill and move away. Betsy thought she caught a glimpse of the boy and Scraps melting into the throng, but when she looked again, they were gone.

"We have scarce been in London a day," her grandmother railed, as she climbed in beside her and sat down stiffly, "and already you've made a spectacle not only of ourselves but a *duke*! Thank God it was His Dottiness, for he's hardly the sort to call Julian out to avenge his dignity. Most likely he will forget the entire incident within a quarter hour, still—"

"His Dottiness?" Betsy blurted.

The countess clapped one hand over her mouth, then warned, "You will forget I said that."

"This instant," Betsy lied earnestly. "Still, I should like to know why you call him that."

"*I* do not—at least I have never done so before— yet Braxton has long been so called among the ton. Never to his face, of course. His mistaking Soho for Piccadilly is an excellent example of why."

"But he was not mistaken, Granmama, for he knew perfectly well—"

"As *I* should have," the dowager interrupted, "when you suggested bringing Boru along. How I let you cajole me into taking him abroad I cannot fathom, yet you'll not get round me again. Henceforth, he will stay at home with George."

The stubborn set of her grandmother's mouth warned Betsy the subject was closed. For the moment, at least.

"I'm sorry, my darling," she whispered to Boru, and laid her head against his warm shoulder.

Though his forgiving whine and affectionate nuzzle gave Betsy a pang of guilt, it also toughened her resolve. Boru loved her, Boru understood.

And Boru hated Julian Dameron.

Chapter Three

It did indeed take less than a quarter hour for Charles Earnshaw to wipe all recollection of the behemoth hound, his mistress, and her termagant grandmother from his mind. It took, in fact, less than five minutes, all the time required by the coachman, Fletcher, to have them under way again, and for Charles to lose himself once more in his book.

The loss was only partial, however, for the cacophony of city sounds drifting through the open window made it difficult to concentrate. He far preferred to keep himself at Braxton Hall, where the peace and solitude of the countryside made it possible to immerse himself totally in his scholarly pursuits.

To him, London was an irritant, an unrelenting distraction, a terrible temptation he longed to, but dared not indulge, for the Earnshaw family tree leaned heavily toward excess. Early on Charles had recognized the tendency in himself and realized he must choose; he could be a bon vivant or he could be a scholar, but he couldn't be both.

He'd chosen the latter without regret. Except upon days such as this, he thought, as he lifted his head from his book to gaze out the carriage window. On days this fine, the splash of sunlight upon the carriages and horses crowding the streets, the busy throngs moving briskly along the flagways, the smells and sights of the vibrant city made him wish—

" 'Ere we are then, Yer Grace. Piccadilly at last."

Fletcher's jovial announcement and the creak of the carriage door as he opened it startled Charles out of his reverie in time to save his book from sliding off his lap. Setting it aside on the banquette, he leaned forward to read the address over the coachman's head: No. 187.

"Why the devil have you brought me to Hatchard's?" he asked, and then remembered. "Oh—never mind, Fletcher."

Charles straightened and began fishing in his pockets. That he'd given his coachman this direction and then promptly forgot doing so was not out of character for him, but his inability to find the scrap of paper upon which he'd written the titles of the books on Roman antiquities given him by Simpson's colleague at the museum was. He searched three times through his pockets, then gave up with an exasperated glance at Fletcher.

"Did I, by any chance, give you a folded bit of paper?"

"No, Yer Grace. Y'did not."

"Damn and blast, I've lost it then!" Charles slapped his left hand on his knee, which drew his attention to his torn sleeve and the cuff creeping over his hand. "And I think I know how," he muttered, then said aloud, "To my mother's house, Fletcher. I can hardly return to the museum like this."

Not that any of the ton would think it strange to

see him striding blithely about with a rip as wide as the Serpentine in his sleeve, but Charles felt he'd done enough for one day to perpetuate the myth of His Dottiness. It had been a near thing with Lady Clymore's granddaughter, but no real harm had been done beyond the clout she'd given him with her reticule. As he raised his hand to rub his jaw, he decided the chit was, without a doubt, the most lethal female he'd ever met.

Every bit as dangerous as her monstrous pet, yet there'd been that initial keen spark in her violet eyes that Charles had taken for intelligence. He knew now that it was menace. Capricious and most likely unintentional, but menace none the less.

Disappointing but fortuitous, otherwise she might very well have caught his slip. The countess hadn't, he was sure. But the incident was a warning, a reminder that he must constantly be on his guard, for the longer he stayed in London, the stronger the temptations would become.

Yet it made no sense to repair to the hall only to return within a fortnight for Lesley's wedding. And there was the matter of the coin, which had brought him to town much earlier than planned, and which could not be dealt with until Simpson returned from Paris. Charles thought about it a moment and decided he would stay. Not for the sake of convenience, but to test his resolve and self-discipline.

Though he was putting up at her house as he always did when in London, he needn't worry about his mother. It had been at least two Seasons since she'd even thought to throw a marriageable miss at his head, and she presently had Lesley's wedding to occupy her. Content that at last he'd convinced his mother and the rest of the ton that he really was somewhat dotty, Charles smiled as he recalled the first time he'd heard the sometimes apt—but nonetheless odious—His Dottiness whispered in his wake as he'd passed through White's.

He'd been outraged, but on the verge of calling out the offending wit, it occurred to him that perhaps this was the answer to a prayer. His ducal responsibilities took far too much time away from his studies, and the endless plague of invitations and females upon his person—not only his mother but other matrons of the ton determined to marry their daughters to a duke, *any* duke—left him feeling like a hunted animal. What better way, he'd decided, to put them all off his trail?

It had been so damnably easy, he marveled that he hadn't thought of it before. His singlemindedness and preoccupation with his studies resulted in a natural forgetfulness that had started the ton calling him His Dottiness in the first place. All he'd had to do was play that up from time to time, and the wags and gabblemongers had seen to the rest.

So kind of them, really, and so clever of Charles. He smiled again, congratulating himself on his cunning as the carriage rolled to a stop in front of his mother's Bond Street mansion and Fletcher opened the door. Then, as the coachman placed the steps, a gust of wind sent the note Charles had written himself at the museum skittering up from the floor.

Where, he thought irritably as he plucked it out of the air, it must have fallen when he'd been attacked by the hound from hell. He couldn't recall the beast's name, but decided Cerberus suited it quite well, even though it lacked the three heads possessed by the mythological dog that guards the mouth of hell. Unless one considered the heads belonging to its mistress and her grandmother.

Smiling at the analogy, Charles alighted his carriage, mounted the steps to the house, and retired to the library, kindly ceded him by his mother for the length of his stay in town. There, safe from temptation, he spent an uninterrupted several days tinkering with this invention, ruminating on that scientific thesis. Quite happily, he thought, until the afternoon when Denham, the butler, rapped on the door.

"Your Grace," he said, once he'd been granted admission, "as she was leaving just now, Her Grace asked me to remind you not to forget to eat."

Charles blinked, startled and caught short. The only flaw in His Dottiness was the occasional moment such as this. Had something his alter ego set into motion slipped his mind or had he genuinely forgotten to dine? Charles tried, but simply could not recall, and was forced to ask cautiously of Denham, "Have I?"

"No, Your Grace, which I told Her Grace. She was quite pleased to hear it."

"Oh, good." He sighed relievedly. "Well, thank you, Denham."

The butler bowed and turned to leave, but Charles called him back. "Denham, did my mother take her leave from her morning room?"

"Yes, Your Grace."

"Why, then, did she not inquire of me as she passed by?"

"I wouldn't know, Your Grace, other than Her Grace was in something of a hurry. She has been at sixes and sevens since she misplaced her engagement book."

How odd. Charles had never known his mother to mislay so much as a hairbrush. "Do you know her direction?"

"Not precisely, Your Grace. Nor did Her Grace, though she believed she had an appointment with her modiste."

Stranger still, thought Charles.

That evening, when he entered the dining room for supper, there was only one place set at the head of the elegantly appointed table and only Denham waiting to attend him.

"My mother?" he inquired.

"Her Grace is dining with Lord and Lady Hampton, Your Grace."

Charles blinked at him. "Who?"

"The Lady Amanda's parents, Your Grace."

"Oh, the Gilbertsons, of course. Wedding plans, I assume."

"I believe so, Your Grace."

Charles sat down and sighed. He was used to dining alone, for he always did at the hall (unless some member of the family was in residence), but in town he was used to company. He thought briefly of calling for his carriage and taking supper at his club, but decided that would be stretching temptation to its limits. Instead he sent Denham to the library for the book he'd been reading, and with it propped open against the candelabra in front of him, felt somewhat less abandoned.

His spirits lifted further, when, on his way back to the library, he encountered his youngest brother, Teddy, dashing down the main staircase into the marble-floored foyer.

"Halfling!" Charles called happily. "There you are!"

"There I *was*," Teddy returned, grinning and tugging on his coat as he downed the last few steps, "for I'm late to the Parkinsons' ball honoring Lesley and Amanda."

"Are you?" Charles asked mildly, noting his black evening dress and the flush in his cheeks. "Mother will be joining you there after the theater, I trust."

"Why, yes," Teddy replied cheerfully, turning toward a gilt-framed mirror hung near the door to fluff his cravat.

"Ted-dy." Charles made two pointed syllables of his name. "Mother is dining with the Gilbertsons."

The boy cringed guiltily in the glass, but recovered almost instantly and heeled about to face Charles. "Are you quite sure? Her engagement book has gone missing, you know."

"I have it straight from Denham." Charles crossed his arms and glowered. "And while we're on it, you little scamp, what do you know about the disappearance of Mother's engagement book?"

"Nothing, I swear," Teddy declared, innocently flattening one palm against his chest.

"I know you too well, halfling." Charles cocked a dubious brow. "It's obvious you're up to your shirt-points in mischief, and it occurs to me how much easier it would be for you if Mother hasn't a clue where *she* is—let alone where *you* are supposed to be. Which, I believe, is upstairs studying your Latin."

"Have a heart, Chas," Teddy begged, looking woebegone. "*She* will be there this evening. So will

Smithers and Forbes—and if *I* am not they'll steal a march on me."

"She?" Charles's eyebrow notched further.

"Yes." Teddy sighed. "The goddess Aphrodite."

More likely a fresh-from-the-schoolroom miss with overlarge blue eyes. The Parkinsons, Charles seemed to recall from his mother's prattling about marriageable females, had two (or was it three?) daughters.

He also seemed to recollect that blue eyes were all the rage just now. It occurred to him to point out that it was not the color of the eyes but what lay behind them—or, perhaps, what did not—that was important, but as he opened his mouth to say so, Teddy pleadingly caught hold of his arms.

"Charles, please . . . She is truly wondrous. Newly come to town and already declared a Beauty *and* an Original. At your age such things must seem somewhat remote, but—"

"My *age?*" he cut in frostily.

"You aren't *quite* ancient," Teddy assured him, though the tone of his voice suggested old age might overwhelm him at any second. "But you are—well—"

" A bit long in the tooth?" Charles put in helpfully. "So decrepit I cannot recall the thrill of romance?"

"It isn't that, so much as it's one thing to be widely read on a subject, yet quite another to experience it firsthand."

"Widely read!" Charles shouted. "See here, I'll have you know that I—"

But in the nick of time, he saw the telltale gleam of mischief in Teddy's green eyes and clamped his mouth shut. Though his mother and Lesley were completely taken in by His Dottiness, Charles had long suspected that sharp-witted Teddy was not.

"Yes, Charles?" he prodded avidly.

Which confirmed that indeed he was *not* fooled by the blustering Charles feigned on the subject of women in order to keep his affairs private. Little wretch, he thought fondly, wishing Teddy would turn his mind to pursuits more worthy than ferreting out his oldest brother's liaisons.

"Never mind. Gentlemen do not discuss such things. And I believe you said you were late."

"You won't tell Mother, will you? I'll devote four hours to my Latin tomorrow evening, I swear."

"Indeed you will, or I'll cart you back to school myself, wedding or no wedding."

"Thank you, Chas!" Teddy gave his shoulders a grateful clasp, then threw open the door. "You are the best of brothers!"

"Old and feeble as I am?" he replied wryly.

"Speaking of that"—halfway through the door, Teddy paused to glance over his shoulder—"the great wits of the ton have altered your nickname, you know."

"Have they?" Charles grinned good-naturedly. "Let me guess. His Twittiness?"

"No, Charles." Teddy shook his head soberly. "They call you His Dodderingness."

"His *what*?" Charles roared, but to the closed door, for Teddy had already shut it in his face. Through the paneled wood, he heard a muffled whoop of laughter, but when he flung the door open, Teddy had vanished into the darkness.

"Little scapegrace," Charles muttered, then slammed the door and stalked back to the library.

Chapter Four

*W*ithin the half hour, Teddy was leaning on one shoulder against a marble pillar in the Parkinsons' ballroom gazing adoringly at Lady Elizabeth Keaton. The diamond brightness of her eyes outshone the shimmering crystal chandeliers, her hair was spun gold, the flush in her cheeks the perfect complement to the petal-pink trim of her gown.

She was the loveliest deb in the room, a fact confirmed by the dozen or so would-be suitors surrounding her. None of them, Teddy was certain, could possibly admire her more than he did, yet Lady Clymore had called him an insolent pup and given him a cuff on the ear when he'd requested an introduction. After it had taken him nearly a sennight to work up the courage.

His ear and his ego smarting, Teddy decided it would be a true pleasure to show the old besom just how insolent a pup he could be. With a devious smile he wheeled off the pillar—and froze at the sight of his mother entering the ballroom with Lord and Lady Hampton. His first thought was that she must have searched his room and found her engagement book, his second to hide before she saw him.

He did so quickly, in a corner screened by an artful arrangement of tropicals from the Parkinsons' orangery. Separating the fronds of a feathery palm, he watched his mother bid good evening to her hostess, start into the room with Lady Hampton, and turn to greet—of all people—the Countess of Clymore.

"Blister it," Teddy muttered, ducking out of sight as the dowager duchess and the dowager countess strolled toward the vacant pair of cut-velvet chairs set before his hiding place.

"Elizabeth is truly lovely, Hesper," he heard his mother say, and shrank lower behind the palms. "To your credit—and to Lydia Parkinson's chagrin it would appear—she has obviously taken."

"Is that silly woman still looking daggers at her?" The belligerent tone of Lady Clymore's voice caused Teddy's ear to throb anew. "I told her a period would shortly be put to Betsy eclipsing her Sarah."

"She's made a match so soon?"

Teddy felt a stab in the region of his heart, and for several moments could hear nothing but the rustle of the ladies' gowns as they seated themselves. Holding his breath, he strained closer, but the countess's reply was further muffled by a nearby trill of laughter.

"But you've always detested the Dameron connection!" his mother declared surprisedly.

"Indeed I still do," her ladyship confirmed heartily, "yet I cannot refuse. He can make his own way, to be sure, for no hostess will refuse the Earl of Clymore. But Julian Dameron is *not*, I assure you, above bruiting it about that I declined to introduce him to Society."

"Then you've no choice," replied the duchess. Teddy heard a faint tapping, which told him his mother was drumming her fan against her chin, a habit she fell into when distracted. "I'd wager he thought all along to follow you to town."

"Though Betsy foretold it, I can scarce credit it," the countess said bitterly. "She warned he would not overlook any opportunity to ruin her chances. And what better way than to drape himself like a millstone about her neck?"

"I'd wager further," the duchess went on, "that he claims to have urgent business in the city."

"Just so," Lady Clymore retorted furiously. "How could I be so easily gulled? Though it is, I suppose, my just desserts for taking the word of a mushroom as that of a gentleman!"

"You've not told Elizabeth?"

"No, and I've no intention. His letter said he will arrive within the week. That's soon enough to pitch her into the dismals."

"Or see her betrothed," the duchess replied pointedly, which sent Teddy's heart plunging.

Chilling as it was to think of the lovely Betsy married to an odious upstart, it was even more maddening to know he could do nothing to prevent it. If he were of age, yes, but three years and two more forms of Latin—which could very well prove to be the death of him—lay between Teddy and his majority.

"A happy thought," the dowager said, with a sigh, "but I fear 'tis impossible in such short time."

"Perhaps not," the duchess said encouragingly. "According to the latest *on-dit*, Elizabeth is the toast of the town."

"And I'll tell you how long that will last," Lady

Clymore predicted sourly. "So long as Betsy can refrain from engaging an exquisite in a discussion of Plato, or until she outrides a whip on Rotten Row. It is merely a question of which will befall her first."

"Oh, my." Teddy heard his mother's fan begin to tap again. "Is she often prone to such mad starts?"

"At least once a day." Her ladyship sighed gloomily. "She has vowed to be on her best behavior, and she will try to be, I know, for she is fundamentally a good gel, but she is a Keaton through and through. The same rash impulse that overcame Edward when he sent his hunter at that impossibly high wall will sooner or later compel his daughter to an act of equal insanity. And I would not put it above Julian Dameron to purposely goad her."

"What the circumstances call for," the duchess replied pragmatically, "is a gentleman of similar interests."

"Do you know of such a one among the ton?"

"Sadly," Eugenia Earnshaw admitted over the *tap tap* of her fan, "I can think of no one at the moment."

But Teddy could. The name and face sprang instantly to mind—along with a plan to save Lady Betsy from the mushroom Dameron—with a brilliance and clarity that left him grinning from ear to ear. It wasn't a perfect match, but half the whole was better than none. And it was the next best thing to offering for her himself.

The plan was not without risks, but no plan worth its salt was. He would have to return his mother's engagement book, but before slipping it into her morning room to be found in plain sight, he would make a few changes and additions to her schedule.

Keeping her haring about town from one mythical appointment to another would make it easier to manipulate clever old Charles, who'd given him the idea in the first place.

His course decided, Teddy straightened, smoothed the tails of his coat, and slipped out from behind the palms. "Good evening to you, Mother," he said, sweeping a deep bow. "And to you, Lady Clymore."

"*You* again!" The dowager snatched up her fan to deliver a smart rap to the back of Teddy's bowed head, but abruptly twisted sideways in her chair to inquire incredulously of the duchess. "This whelp is yours?"

"Sadly, yes," she replied dryly. "May I present my youngest son Theodore."

"Your servant." Teddy bowed again. "With your ladyship's permission, I would pay my addresses to your granddaughter. And with a nod from my mother, I would offer her marriage to save her from this despicable fortune hunter."

Lady Clymore opened her fan and beat furiously at the sudden flush creeping up her throat. "Would you, indeed? What a fine and noble young man you've raised, Eugenia."

The twitching of her lips made it clear she was doing her best not to laugh. Good, good, Teddy thought, shifting his attention and an appropriately pleading look to his mother. One brow was slightly arched, but otherwise her face gave nothing away.

"So it would appear," she said, her voice as nonplussed as her expression. "What do you know of Julian Dameron?"

"Only what I heard her ladyship say," Teddy

blurted. Then added hastily, "Quite by accident, of course."

The duchess smiled, but not pleasantly. "Of course."

"Since I was standing directly behind you," Teddy replied affrontedly, "I could hardly help but overhear."

Her Grace shifted in her chair to glance over her shoulder. When she looked back at Teddy, the arch of her brow had heightened considerably. "How is it I failed to notice you among the palms?"

"A soldier's trick, Mother," he replied loftily. "Lesley taught it to me. Did you know he once evaded a whole Froggie regiment by making himself appear to be part of the shrubbery?"

The duchess's eyelids took a furious leap, but Lady Clymore threw back her head and laughed. So heartily her enormous lavender turban began to tremble.

"By thunder, Eugenia. This is a boy to be proud of! Such a bag of moonshine I've never heard, but it's earned you a dance with my granddaughter." The dowager raised her closed fan and pointed it at him warningly. "Only *one*, mind you, Theodore. I shall be watching."

"Teddy, ma'am, if you please." He grinned at her, then looked imploringly at his mother. "With your permission?"

"Granted, for *one* dance," she replied firmly. "Denied for anything else. If you must beg my leave, you are too young to even think it."

"As Her Grace wishes." Teddy bobbed another quick bow and darted off in the direction of Lady Elizabeth.

"Pity he's such a puppy," Lady Clymore said amusedly. "What do you suppose he's up to?"

"I shudder to even think," replied the duchess, her gaze narrowing speculatively as she watched Teddy thread his way across the crowded ballroom.

That her youngest son was, indeed, up to something Her Grace had every confidence. Beyond the fact that Teddy usually was, there'd been an air of surety about him when he'd made his preposterous offer to Hesper Keaton. He'd known the countess would refuse him, which meant that from the beginning he'd sought only the dance and an opportunity to speak with Lady Elizabeth.

The question, of course, was why. Certainly Teddy was of the right age to be deeply smitten, but Her Grace doubted that was the whole of it. Perhaps a portion of it, she granted, as her gaze shifted thoughtfully toward Betsy. Without question, she was lovely enough to captivate anyone she chose, and at the moment seemed to be doing quite a nice job of enthralling her circle of gallants.

Seemed to be, yes, which was a brilliant complement to her plan, but the glitter in Betsy's eyes was not excitement—any more than the flush in her cheeks was maidenly demure. Confusion was the cause of her high color, and the gleaming pinpoints in her eyes were unshed tears of frustration.

There were names to match the eager faces ringed about her; she knew there were, for she'd been properly introduced to each gentleman. But in the subsequent whirl of waltzes and country dances, she'd been passed from one to the other in such dizzying succession that her head was fairly spinning. She couldn't have said who was who (or was it *whom*?) had her very life depended on it.

If they didn't all go away this instant and give her a chance to collect her wits she was going to scream. Or better yet, take her grandfather's snuff-box out of her small evening reticule and help herself to a pinch. Her fingers itched to do so, but the glimpse she caught through the crowd of her grandmother, beaming beatifically at her from a chair on the sidelines, caused her instead to open her fan, wave it coquettishly, and declare, "Above all things, I believe I would like a glass of punch."

Like a flight of bees, her bevy of admirers broke and made in a perfect wedge for the punch bowl. All but one, a fresh-faced youth with dark hair who stepped out of the throng. He looked scarcely out of leading strings and somehow vaguely familiar, though Betsy was certain she'd never laid eyes on him before.

"Nicely done, Lady Elizabeth," he said admiringly. "If you hadn't called for a glass of punch, I was going to yell, 'Fire!' "

"I wish I'd thought of that," Betsy replied, with a laugh, liking him instantly. That he knew her while she hadn't the foggiest recollection of being introduced to him did not surprise her, yet she felt no embarrassment at admitting the fact. "Forgive me, sir, but I cannot seem to recall your name. I fear I've made too many new acquaintances this evening."

"I am but another, my lady," he replied, with a bow. "I would be honored if you would call me Teddy, but my name is Theodore. Theodore Earn—"

"Teddy it is," she interrupted urgently, as she saw over his bowed head three of her suitors racing toward her with overfull and dripping glasses of punch. "If you will ask me to dance, you may call me Betsy."

By sheer accident, she happened to catch her grandmother's gaze again as she offered her hand, which made the gesture appear as if she were seeking approval. To Betsy's amazement, the dowager nodded, and by the time she recovered from the shock, she and Teddy were on the dance floor moving inexpertly, but carefully, through the steps of a waltz.

"I'm about to speak plainly, my lady, which I hope you will forgive," he said hurriedly, his chin nodding ever so slightly in count with the music, "but your grandmother has allowed me only one dance, and there is much I must tell you. Julian Dameron is arriving in town next week, so we must move quickly."

"That—that—mushroom!" Betsy spluttered furiously. "I *warned* Granmama! I told her he would!"

"So she said, my lady. She said, too, she did not want to upset you, yet I felt you should know. Having the full facts you can—"

"A moment, Teddy, if you please," Betsy cut in. "How is it you know so much of my situation?"

"I overheard Lady Clymore in conversation with my mother. They concur that your best course— perhaps your *only* course—is to make a match before Dameron arrives in London. I quite agree, and I am prepared to come to your assistance."

"You are a *true* gentleman." Betsy patted him gently on the shoulder. "But shouldn't you finish school before you propose marriage?"

"I intend to, my lady," he replied, with a laugh. "But you mistake my meaning. What I meant to say is—"

"I appreciate your concern and your willingness to help," Betsy cut him off again. "But it is quite unnecessary, I assure you. I am not without resources, and I have a plan of my own to thwart my grasping cousin."

"What a happy coincidence, my lady." Teddy grinned good-naturedly. "I, too, have a plan."

Chapter Five

Uncommonly nettled by Teddy's jest, Charles spent a restive evening at his desk in the library. He'd forgiven the little jackanapes by the time he'd retired, but he'd slept poorly, for the rattle of carriages and shouts of the town bucks careening from one entertainment to the next kept him awake most of the night.

Shortly after luncheon the next day, while composing a letter to Simpson about the Roman coin unearthed from a rose bed at the hall by one of the gardeners, Charles nodded off in his chair. Chin on his chest, the reading spectacles forced upon him by a lifetime of prodigious study slipping down his nose, he'd just begun to fall asleep when the squeak of the library door hinges startled him awake.

"Your pardon, Charles." His brother Lesley leaned past the door grinning at him. "I was looking for Mother, but for an awful moment I thought I'd found Papa instead."

"Our father," Charles replied around a stifled yawn, "has been quite dead these last ten years."

"Precisely the point. Have you seen Mother?"

"No!" Charles irritably pulled off his spectacles and glared at Lesley. "And I am *not*, contrary to the latest *on-dit*, anywhere near ready to stick my spoon in the wall!"

"Of course you aren't," Lesley replied mildly. "Who said you were?"

Fully awake now, Charles became aware of how petulant he sounded. "No one of any import," he grumbled. "Only Teddy."

"The little villian." Lesley chuckled and stepped into the room, his curled beaver hat in one hand. "Called you His Dodderingness, didn't he?"

"You've heard it bruited about, too?"

"Only by Teddy, which follows, since he's the great wit who dreamed it up."

"The insolent pup!" Charles flung his spectacles on the desk and sprang to his feet.

"Come down from the boughs, Chas." Lesley laughed and twirled his hat on one finger. "He only means to pry you away from your books. By fair means or foul, he said to me, as well as for your own good. At least for the while you remain in town."

"I see," Charles muttered, his gaze narrowing.

"I did try to dissuade him," Lesley went on, rather unconvincingly, due to the slow spin of the beaver on his finger, "to assure him aren't nearly as shut away from the world as you might appear. But he'd have none of it, and I could scarce tell him about Lady Cromley, could I?"

Charles did his best to look vague. "Tell him what about Lady Cromley?"

"You sly devil." Lesley caught his hat to still it and wagged the index finger of his free hand as he came across the room. "No wonder you've so avidly *embraced* country life."

He gave the word a knowing emphasis that made

Charles's neckcloth, though it was loosely tied, feel suddenly and uncomfortably tight. "I admire Lady Cromley, of course," he replied stiffly, buttoning his waistcoat and wishing he hadn't draped his russet-colored jacket over the back of his chair. "She is, after all, a woman of singular intelligence—"

"And singular beauty." Lesley slid onto a corner of the desk with a wink. "The most lovely widow in the entire parish, I dare say. With absolutely no desire to be a duchess, she assured me."

"Of course she is. And of course she doesn't. Why would she?" Charles demanded in his best toplofty tone. "When did you—er—say you'd seen her?"

"I didn't." Lesley cupped his hat over his bent knee, leaned his forearm on his thigh, and smiled. "But it was just this week past while I was house hunting in the neighborhood for Amanda and me. Vast as the hall is, we've no desire to be underfoot, you know. I met Lady Cromley in the village. She invited me to tea and—"

The library door opened, interrupting him and admitting the Duchess of Braxton. She was frowning and tugging on a pair of blue kid gloves that matched her pelisse and hat ribbons.

"Forgive the intrusion, Charles, but I'm between appointments and—" Her Grace glanced up, saw Lesley perched on the corner of the desk, and her gaze narrowed furiously. "*Here* you are! And where were you yesterday?"

"At Jackson's and at White's. Why?"

"*Why*! Because you were supposed to meet me at Gunter's in Berkeley Square at two of the clock!"

"No, dear. I am to meet you *today* at Gunter's." Lesley laid his hat aside, drew out his pocket watch, and sprang it open as he rose. "And I've purposely come three quarters of an hour early to escort you."

"Then you can escort me to Madame's," the duchess replied imperiously, "for I'm late for a fitting."

"But, Mother," Charles corrected her, "you saw your modiste yesterday, for Denham informed me of it when I asked your direction."

"That's impossible! I *always* see Madame on Wednesday, so I couldn't possibly— Oh, but wait." Her Grace pursed her lips thoughtfully. "Madame could only see me on Tuesday this week. Or was it last?"

"Perhaps you would benefit from the services of a secretary," Charles suggested. "At least until the wedding, or until your engagement book is found."

"And perhaps," his mother retorted, her green eyes beginning to flash, "I would benefit from cooperation rather than criticism. If that is all you have to say, Charles, then kindly return to the library."

"I *am* in the library, Mother," he replied, exchanging a bemused glance with Lesley.

"*More* criticism!" she shrilled, in full cry now. "If you truly wished to be of assistance, you would not spend your every waking moment in this *cursed* room with these *cursed* books! You would lend your time and your person to seeing Lesley and Amanda wed while they are still young enough to fill their nursery! Especially since Caroline Cromley is long past the age of providing you an heir!"

"*Mother!*" Charles and Lesley gasped in shocked unison.

"Forgive my blunt speech, but your father is no longer here to tell you such things so *I* must! You are not quite as clever as you think, Charles, nor is the rest of the world quite so *dim*. But it *is* the outside of enough to hear *you*, who cannot find his boots without his valet, tell me that *I* need a secretary! And furthermore—"

"Mother, see what I've found!" Teddy skidded into the room at a run, pinwheeling his arms to keep from falling on the highly polished floor.

With a graceful sweep of her skirts, the duchess turned and saw her red leather appointment book clutched in one of his madly waving hands. "My engagement calendar!" she cried joyfully, and snatched it away from him.

It was enough to unbalance Teddy and send him thudding to the floor on the seat of his cream-colored trousers. He gave a yelp of pain, but Her Grace stepped nimbly over him with a triumphant smile on her face.

"Now we'll just see, shall we, who is to meet whom and when." She opened her book and read in a lofty tone, as she looked down her nose at the page, "Wednesday the twentieth, Lesley at Gunter's, two of—" Her Grace slapped the book shut with a sniff and squared her shoulders. "Come along then, or we shall be late!"

Kicking her skirts behind her, the duchess sailed out of the room, overstepping her youngest son again without so much as a downward glance. In her wake, Charles and Lesley faced each other, stunned, while Teddy, smothering a satisfied smile, rolled himself over to rub his smarting rump.

"I didn't breathe a word, Chas. I swear it."

"Of course you didn't," replied Charles, his gaze shifting suspiciously toward Teddy.

"And you, halfling?" Lesley turned on his heel, one brow arching speculatively.

"Breathe a word of what?" Teddy asked, levering himself to his feet. "Lady Cromley?"

Out of the mouth of babes, Charles thought, groaning and wiping a hand over his face. Beside him, Lesley made a noise in his throat that could easily pass for a snarl.

"D'you want all of him," he asked Charles, "or should we each take a half?"

"Now see here," Teddy retorted, with an indignant sweep at his mussed hair. "I haven't said a word of anything that Lady Cromley hasn't bruited about herself."

If Teddy had just said he'd passed Latin with flying colors, Charles couldn't have been more stunned. He stood thunderstruck and speechless, until Lesley turned a slow pivot to look at him. "No desire to be a duchess, eh?"

"I fear," Charles replied, the anger and betrayal he felt deepening his voice to a growl, "that the lady doth protest too much."

"I believe you've hit the mark squarely." Lesley gave him a quick but reassuring clap on the shoulder. "You tend to the scamp. I'll speak to Mother."

Swiping his hat off the desk, Lesley strode toward the door, paused there with his hand on the knob, and looked back at Teddy. "A word to the wise, halfling." He pointed his thumb at Charles over his shoulder. "He is the Duke of Braxton and your fate rests in his hands."

"Yes, Lesley," Teddy murmured meekly. He was, in fact, counting on it, and as the library door closed behind Lesley, he turned a suitably contrite face to Charles.

And for an awful moment didn't recognize him, for he'd fully expected to see His Dottiness still standing in a wounded daze behind the desk. The fire in Charles's eyes, the air of immutable authority fairly crackling around him, gave Teddy such a fright the starch nearly went out of his neckcloth. And in the next instant his resolve, when Charles smashed a fist against the desk with such force that the inkwell wobbled.

"Damn and blast it!" he swore viciously.

Prayers Teddy hadn't known he remembered leapt into his head. He murmured them fervently, his lips moving, until Charles hissed between his teeth and flung his hand open to shake it. An audible sigh escaped him then and he grinned, almost giddy with relief, as Charles dropped heavily into his chair and rubbed his hand.

"Let that be a lesson to you, halfling." His eyes were simmering, but no longer blazing. "Emotion never solves anything. Only logic and reason."

"I quite agree," Teddy replied, coming forward to sit in the leather chair before the desk.

"Since when?" Charles raised a brow at him. "Have you turned a new leaf since breakfast?"

"It was made vividly clear to me when Mother and I chanced to meet at the Parkinsons' last evening," Teddy explained gravely. "She cut up rather stiff."

"I did try to warn you." Charles gave up rubbing his hand and leaned tiredly back in his chair. "Wise of you to return her book. Too late, but wise none the less."

"Right you are, Chas." Teddy leaned eagerly forward and bent one elbow on the desk. "I should have listened to you. I should *always* listen to you, and I wish now that I had."

"Never too late to start, halfling." Charles preened, but a second later went stiff and upright as a vicar in his chair. "Cut line, scamp. Out with it."

Teddy blinked naively. "Out with what?"

"Whatever it is you're trying to turn me up sweet before you tell me. Is it what you heard Lady Cromley say?"

"Oh, no, Chas. Nothing of the kind." Teddy lowered his gaze and squirmed in his chair.

"Come now." Charles cleared his throat. "It can't be as bad as all that. If I'm to mollify Mother and avoid a scandal, you must tell me."

"I only heard what she told Lesley," Teddy said, leaving out that he'd heard it just now as he'd listened at the keyhole. "That she had no desire to be a duchess. But it wasn't so much what she said as how she said it, if you take my meaning."

Charles winced, bent his elbow, and pinched the bridge of his nose. "I do."

"Seems a pretty thin broth for scandal, Chas."

"It wouldn't be in town." He frowned and let his hand fall away from his face. "Fortunately Caro loves the country, so she can blather it about the village till she turns blue, or until Lesley and Amanda are wed and I can return to the hall and put a stop to it." The duke's gaze drifted toward the library windows, a perverse smile darkening his features. "Whichever comes first."

"Then it would probably be best," Teddy said soberly, "if I postpone my trip to Gretna until after the wedding."

"Ummm, yes," Charles agreed absently, lifting one hand to rub his chin. "I would if I were you."

"All right, then." Teddy got to his feet. "I'm off to study my Latin. Good day, Chas."

"Ummm," Charles repeated, still rubbing his chin.

Intent on putting as much distance as possible between them, Teddy heeled quickly about and made for the door. He was no more than three steps shy of it when comprehension dawned, and Charles roared, "*Gretna!* I *forbid* it!"

Teddy turned and faced the Duke of Braxton, red-faced and on his feet behind his desk. "That's exactly what Mother said last night when I offered for Betsy."

"I should hope so!" Charles came swiftly around the desk. He opened his mouth to shout something else, but instead he blinked puzzledly and asked, "Betsy who?"

"Lady Elizabeth Keaton," Teddy said, sighing her name rapturously. "The goddess Aphrodite."

Otherwise known as the mistress of the hound from hell.

Though Charles hadn't turned so much as a single thought toward Betsy since the Oxford Street fiasco, her face leapt into his mind with a clarity that alarmed him almost as much as it horrified him. He hadn't realized he'd remembered her name, the vivid blue of her eyes, the sheen of her hair—or the dangerous streak in her nature until now.

"Ah, yes." Charles smiled and folded his arms. "You mentioned her last evening. 'A Beauty and an Original,' I believe you said." A Menace and Bedlamite, he added grimly to himself.

"She's wonderful, Chas. Truly wonderful. D'you

50

know, she said I should finish school before I even think about marriage?" Teddy beamed angelically. "You must meet her. Say you will."

"Oh, I intend to," Charles assured him fiercely. "Just as soon as you give me her direction, and your solemn word that you'll go no farther with this demented plan for elopement until I do."

"If I could, of course I would, but it's quite impossible. Julian Dameron is due in town next week."

"Who the devil is Julian Dameron?" Charles demanded, managing, but just barely, not to shout.

"Betsy's cousin, the Earl of Clymore. Hasn't a feather to fly with, so he's determined to have Betsy and her portion. It's why she's come to London, you see, to escape him—but he's reneged on his agreement not to follow."

"She's come to town, you clunch," Charles retorted bluntly, "for the same reason *every* young miss comes—to find herself a husband!"

"Not Betsy. She doesn't wish to marry anyone. She has the perfect plan to avoid Dameron, though she wouldn't tell me what it is."

"Of course she wouldn't, you chuckle-head!" Charles all but bellowed. "For *you* are the plan!"

"Then why did she refuse my offer?"

"Because she's a cunning little chit, and you are greener than grass if you cannot see it!"

"You are wrong, Chas. You only think so because Lady Cromley has played you false."

"This has nothing to do with—" Charles caught himself in midshout, took a deep breath to calm himself, and went on, a muscle leaping in his jaw. "It may seem to you that I am painting Lady Eliz-

51

abeth with the same brush, but that, too, is due to your lack of age and experience.

"So, unless you wish to be locked in your room with a Latin tutor until you reach your majority, you will give me your word that you have abandoned all thought of marrying anyone—*especially* Lady Elizabeth Keaton—over the anvil."

"You drive a hard bargain, Chas," Teddy complained bitterly, clenching his fists for dramatic effect, "but you have my word."

"Very well, then." Charles gave him a stiff nod of dismissal. "You have my leave to go."

Teddy took it and went, but only as far as the corridor outside the library. There, as he pulled the door shut behind him, he peered through the crack and saw Charles distractedly pacing the room, one hand on his hip, the other raking repeatedly through his hair.

"No desire to be a duchess," he muttered under his breath. "No wish to wed anyone, indeed!"

"Oh, Chas?" Teddy pushed the door inward a bit and leaned his head inside the library. "I've recalled another remark I heard Lady Crom—"

"Not now, halfling," Charles cut him off. "One scheming female at a time."

"As you wish," he murmured, and eased the door shut.

Grinning gleefully, Teddy took himself up to his room and the Latin grammar waiting for him on the writing table before the windows. With a pen knife drawn from his pocket, he peeled away the stiff backing on the inside cover, withdrew a sheet of Charles's crested stationery filched from his desk in the library at Braxton Hall, then carefully resealed his hiding place, and laid the book aside.

"My dearest Caro," he murmured ardently, still grinning as he dipped his pen in the well and sat down to write.

His imitation of Charles's sketchy script was flawless, made perfect by years of forging replies to notes intercepted from his masters. The key was haste, for the Duke of Braxton's thoughts always outpaced his hand. Scarce a minute and three quarters later, the seconds ticked off by the pocket watch inscribed to him by Charles on his last birthday, which lay on the table beside him, the note was penned, sanded, and secreted in his pocket.

Recalling the smash of Charles's fist against the desk, Teddy suffered a momentary qualm of doubt as he pictured a fiery-eyed and furious Duke of Braxton swooping down unaware on the lovely Lady Betsy. Only once before, when the solution to a mathematical equation had eluded him for several days, had he ever seen Charles so angry.

But a storm was sometimes necessary, Teddy reasoned, to lift a becalmed ship from the doldrums. And Lady Elizabeth Keaton was, he felt sure, the perfect tempest, her wit and resolve equal to Charles at his most formidable.

Should all else fail, though Teddy didn't think for an instant it would, there was her wonderful reticule full of oddments, one or two of which she'd shown him the night before. The memory brought a wickedly happy smile to his face as he pocketed his watch, fixed the fob to his waistcoat, and went out to post the note inviting Lady Cromley to London.

Chapter Six

*U*naccustomed as he was to evening dress, Charles was quite accustomed to being stared at upon entering a room. So accustomed, in fact, that he scarcely noticed the sudden glare in Lady Pinchon's ballroom caused by the dozens of quizzing glasses lifted surprisedly in his direction.

Nor did he sense the faint stir of air. Had he noticed the doors leading to the garden were shut against the evening chill, he might have guessed the reason—the plethora of fans snapped suddenly open by madly whispering dowagers—but he did not, for he was intent only on locating Lady Elizabeth Keaton, putting paid to her designs on Teddy, and getting the blazes out of here as quickly as possible.

By the thinness of the crowd he judged it would not take long, which suited his eardrums as well as his purpose. The walls were fairly vibrating with the loudness of the music, for Lady Pinchon was nearly as deaf as the marble columns supporting the ceiling. Already the fortissimo country dance was giving him a headache, but Charles set his jaw against it and moved out of the doorway.

So far this was the third Society affair he'd graced in search of Lady Elizabeth. She and her grandmother had managed to stay at least a quarter of an hour ahead of him and the dozen or so pinks of the ton who'd been in hot pursuit of her all evening.

There'd been near collisions and neck-and-neck races from one establishment to the next, which Fletcher had kept them out of at Charles's insistence. Not because it was unseemly for a duke, but because the temptation of the chase set his blood singing dangerously. Emotion never solves anything, he'd told Fletcher, only logic and reason.

Both of which threatened to fail Charles as he caught sight of his quarry, already run aground by the pack of young bucks he'd been trailing all evening. Scheming chit, he thought darkly, helping himself to a glass of champagne offered by a passing footman. She tipped back her head to laugh at some amusing remark as he watched her, the gleam of the chandeliers winking in the facets of the small diamond choker circling her throat. She'd hooked her fish, yet she was still casting lures.

Or so it seemed to Charles, while Betsy was enjoying herself immensely. Thanks to the bits of lamb's wool she'd brought along in her small evening reticule and stuffed in her ears to save them from the overloud music, she couldn't hear a single syllable uttered by her noisome suitors. Hopefully, since her plan to evade them by whisking herself and her grandmother from one engagement to the next hadn't worked, she was laughing at the most inappropriate comments and convincing them she was a total shatterbrain.

Rash young fools, Charles thought scornfully of the gallants surrounding Betsy. To go haring off after a pretty face, to risk life and cattle to bask in the glow of a dazzling smile, to be the first to lead a Beauty out for a waltz ... to be two and thirty and never have done any of those things.

The thought leapt unbidden into his head, with such ferocity that the stem of the goblet in his hand snapped cleanly in two. Champagne spilled over his fingers and he blinked at them, stunned, then looked hastily up in search of a footman, only to lock his gaze with Lady Elizabeth's, just as she laughingly tossed her head in his direction.

She froze, but only for a heartbeat, long enough for her eyes to take a startled leap from his face to the shattered goblet in his hand. Then her lashes swept down and she turned away. Still laughing, Charles noted, feeling gauche and ridiculously angry.

Murmuring apologies, a footman appeared and took the shards. Irritably Charles pulled out his handkerchief to wipe his hand and wondered what the devil was wrong with him. The champagne, he decided. He was hardly foxed, yet he'd drunk more this evening than he had in the past six months. All in pursuit of the scheming little minx who had the audacity to laugh at him.

But she was not alone, Charles realized, intercepting several sidelong glances aimed in his direction. He returned them disdainfully, and noticed that like Lady Pinchon, most of her guests were well advanced in years. Were they sniggering at His Dottiness, he wondered sourly, or His Dodderingness?

Never mind that the nickname existed only in Teddy's head, it rankled. Nearly as much as the realization that he shouldn't have come, that what he had to say was best said in private, perhaps even to the dowager countess rather than her granddaughter. He'd reacted rashly, without thought, purely from emotion. He'd fallen victim to temptation, not champagne.

But it occurred to Charles, as he watched Lady Elizabeth open her fan, that he could trap her with her own snare. Acting rashly again, and quite forgetting his mother's caution that he was not as clever as he thought, Charles gave his waistcoat a tug, squared his unpadded shoulders, and stepped boldly forward to join the hunt.

Having kept the Duke of Braxton in wary view since the flash of breaking glass had caught her attention, Betsy saw him approach her grandmother and felt her pulse quicken. He'd not forgotten her, that much was clear from the unnerving stare he'd kept trained upon her for the last several minutes. The intensity of his gaze had made her shiver and turn away, yet she'd remained aware of his unwavering attention. Had he come seeking restitution for the incident in Oxford Street? Or satisfaction?

Much as she despised Julian, Betsy had no wish to see him shot or run through by the Duke of Braxton. If she could escape him no other way, she'd wield the pistol or rapier herself, thank you very much. Not that it hadn't been kind of her new young friend Teddy to offer, but—

A gasp of recognition caught in Betsy's throat as she watched the duke bow over her grandmother's hand and turn to face her. Braxton's eyes were more blue than green, but the thick dark hair gleaming like a raven's wing in the candlelight, his straight nose, and square jaw were the same as Teddy's. Were they cousins or brothers? Betsy wondered, sinking quickly into a curtsey as the duke approached and her suitors gave way.

"Good evening, Your Grace," Betsy murmured, rising as he completed his bow to her.

"Lady Elizabeth," he said, offering his elbow. "Your grandmother has given me permission for this waltz."

At least that's what Betsy thought he said, for she couldn't quite hear him, but his proferred arm and a hasty glance at her grandmother's beaming face seemed to confirm it. Her pulse quickening, Betsy laid her hand on the Duke of Braxton's wrist. It was trepidation, she told herself, not excitement at being led onto the dance floor by the youngest, handsomest duke in the realm.

"So, my lady," Charles began, once he had the little conniver firmly in his grasp. "Are you enjoying London?"

"Oh, yes, Your Grace," Betsy returned, striving vainly to hear him. He'd said London, she thought.

"Have you made many conquests?" Charles asked blandly.

Was that something about the country? Did she prefer it to the city? "Oh, no, Your Grace." Betsy smiled dazzlingly, wishing fervently she could make out what he was saying.

"Really?" Charles queried mildly. The little baggage, he thought contemptuously. "You seemed quite surrounded just now."

Had he said round or ground? Betsy cast a frantic look about her for a clue and saw nothing rounder than the plump pink cherubs painted on the frescoed ceiling. Surely *not*, she thought, flushing to the roots of her hair.

She colored most becomingly, Charles owned, but

cynically. Certain now that he was near to cracking her facade, he pressed bitingly, "How well are you acquainted with my brother, my lady?"

"Why *no*, Your Grace," Betsy assured him, "it's no bother at *all* to dance with you."

Charles came to an abrupt, stone-footed halt fortuitously near the doorway and out of the path of the other dancers. "I beg your pardon?"

Her eyes, brilliant as the diamonds at her throat, were the only color left in Betsy's face. Swiftly, as if his touch burned, she withdrew from his arms.

"My grandmother would have my head if I slapped you," she returned scathingly, "but someone *should*, Your Grace, for even *thinking* I would accompany you to the garden!"

"I said *pardon*!" Charles exclaimed indignantly, but to her back, for she'd already swept haughtily away from him. Aware that heads were turning in their direction, he hurried after her, caught her by the elbow, and spun her around in the doorway. "I said *nothing* about the garden! I said—"

"Unhand me," Betsy said icily, "or I will scream."

Charles did so, let her pass through the archway into the foyer beyond, then leapt after her and reclaimed her elbow. He also put his right foot firmly down on the hem of her gown—but remained angrily oblivious to it as he again pulled her around to face him.

"Now see here, young lady. Your ploys and poses will not work with me. I am not a green boy to be led about—"

"Oh, bother!" With her free hand, Betsy plucked the lamb's wool from her ears. "Now that I can hear, kindly deliver your setdown and leave me in peace!"

How perfectly brilliant, Charles thought, totally forgetting Teddy in his amazement and admiration of her ingenuity. What a simply clever defense against permanent ear damage. "Tell me, my lady," he said eagerly. "Were you able to hear anything I said?"

"No," Betsy confirmed distastefully. "Not clearly, at any rate—for which I shall be eternally grateful."

Then she hadn't been laughing at him, Charles realized, taking in her overbright eyes and defiantly lifted chin. He further supposed that with her ears stuffed with wool, she could very easily have mistaken *pardon* for *garden*. How utterly famous, he marveled, struck by the irony and yet pleased beyond reason that she'd meant to slap him. So very pleased that he laughed.

So suddenly and so heartily that mirthful tears sprang in his eyes. And in Betsy's, too, though she felt anything but merry. She felt murderous. And mortified to be laughed at by a duke, no matter how dotty he pretended to be. He wasn't, of course—at least, she hadn't thought so—but the abrupt change in his demeanor was beginning to make her wonder. Ripping into her one moment, howling with glee the next, and now, to Betsy's utter astonishment, breaking off to purse his lips and tap one finger against his chin.

"A denser substance would have served you better," he said thoughtfully. "Something moldable that could be easily shaped to fit the ear. May I suggest candlewax? I believe it would be just the thing."

"So would throttling you!" Betsy declared, lifting her skirts to wheel away from him, unaware until she'd taken a step and felt the *r-i-i-p* at her waist that the deeply ruffled flounce of ice-blue satin that made the hem of her gown was trapped beneath the Duke of Braxton's foot.

She froze, horrified, feeling a chill race up the backs of her legs to take the place of the satin panel billowing away from her. Betsy felt it float past her knees, felt the color drain from her face, saw her reputation and her future being torn to shreds along with her gown.

Charles saw the same picture, his own clumsy part in it, and but one way to save her. Of the snowy petticoat her grandmother had insisted she wear to ward off the chill night air, he had only a glimpse as he snatched up the fluttering panel, looped his left arm around her waist, pulled her against him, and felt her go rigid with shock and insult.

"Let me go!" she cried, aghast.

"Would you prefer the world and all his wife to see your petticoat?" Charles retorted, glancing swiftly about. The foyer was mercifully empty, and the avid audience they'd had near the ballroom doorway had returned their attention to the dancers.

"I would prefer you release me," Betsy shot contemptuously over her shoulder, "before you shred my reputation along with my gown!"

"Then stop behaving like a widgeon and allow me to assist you," Charles replied pragmatically. "Walk quickly to the door and you may yet save your virtue."

Despite her fury and embarrassment, Betsy had sense enough to realize it was the only logical course. Steeling herself against the duke's scandalous embrace, she moved swiftly forward. So abruptly that Charles was hard put to keep pace with her, keep the torn panel between them with a hand at the small of her back and his arm about her waist.

Since Lady Pinchon's great age had forced her to move the ballroom to the ground floor, they had scarce thirty feet to cover to reach the entrance, the darkness beyond, and safety. A paunchy footman in powdered wig and livery merely bowed at their shocking in-tandem approach and opened the door.

As they swept past, Charles commanded him to summon the dowager countess. To the footman stationed between potted topiaries in the chilly, torchlit dark beneath the portico, he said, in the voice that had moved Teddy to prayer, "The Clymore carriage, this moment."

The servant bowed hastily and scurried away. Catching the torn panel between his teeth, Charles removed his jacket. Studiously keeping his gaze locked on the back of Lady Elizabeth's golden head, he eased it about her waist.

"Thank you, Your Grace," she said tightly, as she took the sleeves from him and tied them into a firm knot.

"You see, my lady? All's well that ends well." Charles held the panel of her skirt between his outstretched hands and wryly arched an eyebrow. "With the exception, I fear, of your gown."

His lofty, bemused tone was too much. Overcome by embarrassment, anger, and her rash Keaton temperament, Betsy rounded on the Duke of Braxton like a flash of lightning and began thrashing him with the fan draped over her wrist by its thin gold cord.

Taken by surprise, Charles flung up his arms to fend her off. The sight of her skirt panel still stretched between his hands drew a shriek from Betsy and a fresh volley of blows, most of which landed harmlessly on the length of pale satin. When she'd exhausted her strength and her breath, Charles lowered his shield and looked at her.

She glared back at him, her bosom heaving, her furious gaze burning more intently than the torch-light flickering on her flushed cheeks. Her coiffure was a tangled mass of curls gleaming like spun gold in the smoky glow.

"Keep away from me." Pointing her battered fan like a pistol, Betsy backed away from him. "You are a mad, rag-mannered menace!"

"Your servant." Charles bowed, neither surprised nor unpleased to note that His Dottiness's fame had preceded him. "I would be delighted to give my lady a wide berth." He folded her skirt panel and offered it to her. When she reached for it, he snatched it out of her grasp. "In exchange for a small favor."

"Name it."

"You have my word that I will ignore your very existence if you will agree to cut my brother Teddy from your circle of suitors." Charles offered the panel again and was surprised to see her hesitate.

"It was *brother* you said, not *bother*, wasn't it?" she asked, a wary, almost wounded tone in her voice.

"Indeed it was. Do we have an agreement?"

Betsy could scarce believe he was serious. "What

on earth makes you think I would consider Teddy an eligible *parti*?"

"It has been my experience," Charles replied curtly, "that any male in long pants is considered fair game during the Season."

"And you think me on the hunt, Your Grace?" Betsy inquired icily.

"Do you deny it?"

"Most vehemently!"

"As did Teddy. But I am not an impetuous boy who is so easily convinced."

"Indeed you are not, Your Grace! You are an arrogant, insufferable—" Betsy began furiously, but was cut short by the sudden opening of the door.

Light from the chandeliers and her harried-looking grandmother tumbled onto the steps of Lady Pinchon's house. "God's teeth!" the dowager squawked, her startled gaze leaping from Charles to Betsy and back again. "What's happened now?"

"Nothing serious, Lady Clymore," Charles assured her. "As the seam of my coat failed me in Oxford Street, so the stitches in Lady Elizabeth's gown have failed her."

"Them dem Frenchie modistes!" the dowager exclaimed, blustering her way to Betsy's side. "It's their revenge for Boney, I swear it is!"

The clatter of hooves announcing the arrival of the Clymore carriage drew Charles's attention from her ladyship's clucking and fussing to the splendid grays drawing the shiny barouche to a halt beneath the portico. The coachman, an unlit pipe clamped in his teeth, cast a baleful eye on Charles as a broad-limbed footman swung down from the rear to open the door and place the steps.

"George!" Lady Clymore commanded. "Fetch our wraps!"

"Yes, m'lady," the footman replied, shooting Charles a less than respectful glance as he passed him on the steps.

These servants are as brazen as their mistress, Charles marveled, noting that the coachman had wrapped one hand in readiness about his whip. He noticed, too, that Lady Elizabeth, her nose in the air and pointedly ignoring him, was gathering what was left of her skirts and preparing to mount the carriage steps behind her grandmother.

"Not so fast, my lady." Charles moved quickly to intercept her. "I would have your answer."

He offered his arm to assist her as was polite, but Lady Elizabeth refused it. Instead, she faced him with a defiantly lifted chin and a barely civil curtsey.

"I am flattered, Your Grace, that you think me such a threat," she said in a scathing tone. "And my answer is that both you and your brother can go to the devil!"

Then she snatched her skirt panel away from him, stomped up the steps into the carriage, and slammed the door in his face.

Chapter Seven

"Why was I born *female*?" Betsy fumed for at least the hundredth time since breakfast, as she paced the apple green and cherry pink morning room. "If I were a man I could have called him out for such an insult!"

On the rug by the hearth, where a fire burned against the autumn chill, Boru raised his head hopefully and thumped his tail as his mistress stalked past him. That, too, for at least the hundredth time.

"No gentleman," Lady Clymore replied, without looking up from her embroidery, "would credit such a challenge."

"And why not?" Betsy demanded, halting near the windows to glare at her grandmother. The sun had nearly melted the rime of frost from the glass and shot her golden hair with silver highlights.

"If you *were* a man," the countess replied, peering over the spectacles she wore to ease the strain of needlework, "would *you* be able to keep a sober face if summoned to the field of honor by a young hothead named Elizabeth?"

"*If* I were a man," Betsy returned, her hands thrust on her hips, "I would not be Elizabeth. I would be Edward after Father and Grandfather."

"And well on your way to rack and ruin," Lady Clymore retorted, then added lightly, hoping to jolly Betsy out of her foul temper, "And you would look monstrous silly in green-sprigged muslin."

"This is not a subject for jest, Granmama. That odious man insulted me!"

"That odious man is a duke I will remind you for the last time. And he did no more than state the truth. You have in fact come to town to find a husband."

"Because I am female!" Betsy declared, throwing her arms wide. "Do you not see the injustice?"

"I see it, but am powerless to change it." Lady Clymore laid her embroidery aside, removed her spectacles, and saw that Betsy in her beseeching, sunlit pose looked like a grievously maligned and very angry angel. "I also see by the clock that it is nearly time for morning calls, and advise you to come down from the boughs lest you give the gentlemen whose bouquets fill the Blue Saloon a disgust of you."

"And that is another thing!" Betsy snatched up a handful of cards and notes that had come with the floral tributes. "I haven't the dimmest notion who any of these gentlemen are! How am I to find a companionable husband among my dancing partners when I am passed from one to the other in such a whirl that I scarce remember *my* name, let alone theirs?"

"That is the whole idea, you silly gel." Her ladyship tugged exasperatedly at the silk paisley shawl laid over her shoulders as she sprang to her feet from a velvet settee. "If given sufficient opportunity to think about it and become acquainted, no young person of any sense—either male *or* female—

would ever marry anyone and the population would suffer a serious decline!"

"A splendid notion!" Betsy tossed the cards in the air, folded her arms, and glared at her grandmother. "It will save the world from future tyrants such as the Duke of Braxton!"

Like leaves tossed on a feckless wind, the notes penned on the finest velum skittered toward the floor, stirring Boru from his rug with a yap of excitement. He snapped one out of the air, thoroughly mangling it in his great jaws before bringing it to Betsy and plopping it, wet with drool and crumpled beyond redemption, at her feet.

The dowager fell back on the settee with a groan and a hand over her eyes, but at last, Betsy laughed. Dropping to one knee, she put her arms around Boru and hugged his warm, shaggy neck. He whined and banged his tail happily against one leg of a small table.

The hand-painted china shepherdess and her flock placed there trembled and tottered precariously toward the edge. The delicate figurines were a particular favorite of her ladyship, and one of the few items the staff had missed on their sweep of the house before her arrival with Betsy and the "beast," as Boru was called by the servants.

If Iddings had not, at that moment, appeared in the doorway with Charles's coat wrapped in tissue and folded in a box, Little Bo-Peep and her sheep would have fallen victim to the Irish wolf. The quick-witted butler scarce had time to toss the package into a chair, lift the hem of his green baize apron, and slide onto his knees to catch them as they toppled off the edge.

At the thump on the carpet beside her, Betsy

drew away from Boru, saw Iddings with a relieved expression on his face and her grandmother's cherished china flock in his apron. Quickly she snatched them up and dashed them to safety on the mantle. Boru followed her, while Iddings gingerly pinched the ruined note off the floor and disposed of it in the fire.

When Lady Clymore uncovered her eyes, she saw Betsy warming her hands at the hearth, Boru stretched on the rug, and her majordomo holding a box and waiting in the doorway to be acknowledged. "Yes, Iddings?"

"The Duke of Braxton's coat, my lady, sponged and pressed as you requested."

"Excellent." The dowager rose from the settee with her spectacles in hand and moved to her writing table. "I shall just pen a note, then you may send it by footman to the residence of the dowager duchess in Bond Street."

While her grandmother seated herself and inked a quill, Betsy lifted her gaze from the fire screen to Iddings. Gratitude shimmered in her eyes as she mouthed the words, "Thank you." Touched by her kindness and the unexpected acknowledgement, Iddings gave her a bow and a smile, then hastily resumed an impassive countenance as Lady Clymore bent one elbow on the back of her chair.

"A brief line of thanks from you would be neither untoward nor misconstrued, I think," she said to her granddaughter.

The stern look she offered along with the curved goose feather gave Betsy no choice. Reluctantly she moved to the writing table and took the quill and the chair from her grandmother.

"Keep in mind that you are writing to a duke of the realm."

A very learned duke if what Teddy had told her of his oldest brother could be trusted. Smiling, Betsy dipped the quill in a silver well, wrote two flourishing lines in Latin and her name beneath her grandmother's cramped signature.

"What does this say?" Lady Clymore snatched the paper from the table and peered at it through her spectacles.

"That I am most grateful to His Grace for his kind assistance," Betsy lied, with her very best and most guileless expression, "and that I shall humbly endeavor never to trouble him again."

The dowager looked pointedly down her nose as she returned the note to her granddaughter to be sanded and sealed. "Which of course you shall not."

That much at least Betsy could guarantee, for what she'd written to His Grace was that he possessed the manners of a goat, and if he did not keep to his word as a gentleman to henceforth ignore her very existence she would never release Teddy from her snare. A far cry from calling him out, but it would do.

"Here you are, Iddings." The countess took the finished note from Betsy and held it out to the butler as he crossed the room to take it. "Kindly send George to collect Boru for his exercise. I believe it best that he be absent during morning calls."

"Yes, my lady." Iddings tucked the note inside the box, bowed, and took his leave.

Slapping the flat of her hand on the table, Betsy wheeled to her feet to face her grandmother. "Must you banish Boru at every turn?"

"So long as he continues to be a menace, yes."

Lady Clymore snatched off her spectacles and shook them emphatically at Betsy. "Don't think me a blind or easily gulled old fool, my gel. If not for Iddings, my dear little shepherdess—" Her spectacles froze in midwag and her eyes widened with realization and alarm. "Iddings!" she cried, rushing past Betsy. "Bring that box to me at once!"

The dowager turned sharply through the doorway to the left, her shawl billowing behind her like a sail. Betsy threw a panicked glance at Boru, lying on the hearth rug with his ears pricked and his head cocked curiously.

"I'm in the sauce now for sure," she told him, then hiked up her skirts and bolted for the door, reaching it in time to see the fringed hem of her grandmother's shawl disappear around the turn at the head of the passageway that led to the foyer.

"Iddings! Do not open that door!"

Envisioning the countess throwing herself bodily on the butler to prevent delivery of the box and the note, Betsy charged after her, unaware that Boru loped behind her and that George had burst through the kitchen door at the far end of the passageway. Alarmed by the dowager's screech, the sight of Betsy's raised skirts and flashing ankles was all the provocation the footman needed to follow at a run.

Where the passageway ended, so did the thick gold runner. Forced to slow her pace or fall on the gleaming marble, Betsy lowered her skirts and grasped the curved wall of the archway to break her momentum. If Boru hadn't misjudged the footing she might have managed a breathless but ladylike appearance in the mouth of the foyer. But just as she swung herself into the open, Boru's front

71

paws hit the highly polished floor and shot out from under him.

He careened off the wall with a yelp and smacked squarely into Betsy. Her feet and her skirts flew up and she fell with a shriek, mostly on top of Boru. Grasping handfuls of his shaggy coat, she hung on for dear life as they went sliding across the foyer, her eyes tightly closed, until they spun to a stop against a pair of sturdy legs.

The jolt snapped Betsy's head back and opened her eyes to the upside-down faces of Iddings and her grandmother. Their stricken, glassy-eyed expressions reminded Betsy of jack-o'-lantern grins—and sent a chill up her back as she realized they were not looking at her.

Several curls loosened from the stylish knot pinned to her crown tumbled over her eyes as Betsy lowered her head, but she had no trouble recognizing the gilt-haired man framed in the open doorway in front of her. *"Julian!"*

"Elizabeth," the Earl of Clymore replied, his voice as chilly as the sunlight filtering past him into the foyer. "Your life is in chaos as usual, I see."

With difficulty, Betsy stifled an angry retort. Though it hardly seemed possible, Julian was even higher in the instep than he'd been when last they'd met at Clymore. He stood looking down at her, not at her face, but at her very shapely and very exposed legs.

There was no admiration in his gaze, only disapproval, still Betsy hurriedly tucked up her knees and pulled down her skirts, uncovering Boru to Julian—and Julian to Boru. Man and hound stared at each other, startled and unblinking, until Boru shook himself free of her petticoats and lunged with a growl and bared fangs.

"Boru, no!" Betsy grasped his collar and pulled with all her might, but she was no match for the hound's great strength.

If George hadn't clamped his thick, muscled hands on either side of her and pulled Boru back, the Earl of Clymore would have been his midday meal. His fangs snapped shut on thin air rather than Julian's right knee, and Betsy went limp with relief.

So did the earl. So limp and so pale that he might've swooned, Betsy thought, if her grandmother hadn't stepped quickly forward to thump him on the back as George hauled the still snarling dog a safe distance away.

"Betsy has been training Boru to guard the house," Lady Clymore told him cheerfully. "Capital job, don't you think?"

The dowager's amazing defense of Boru brought Betsy to her feet—and the color flooding back to Julian's face. "More likely," he said darkly, his pale blue eyes narrowing with fury as they settled on Boru, "a capital job of trying to kill me."

In George's strong hands, Boru had stopped snarling and merely stared balefully at Julian. Arrogant and insufferable as he was, he was still the Earl of Clymore. A word from him and Boru would suffer a fate worse than banishment.

And so would Julian, Betsy vowed, as she forced a gay laugh. "Don't be silly," she said, slipping her arm through his to draw him away from the door so Iddings could close it. "Why on earth would I do such a thing?"

"I can think of several reasons," Lady Clymore muttered, ducking her chin to fuss with her shawl.

"I beg your pardon, my lady?" Julian's gaze shifted from Boru to the dowager countess. His voice was mild, but his eyes had narrowed another fraction.

"I said we did not expect to see you in town for the Little Season." Her ladyship raised her chin and one eyebrow imperiously. "In fact, I believe I had your word that we would not."

"I have urgent business in the city," the earl replied, just as imperiously, as he gave his beaver hat and walking stick to Iddings. "To do so without calling upon you would be most rude."

"Indeed." Lady Clymore's brow arched higher. "T'would also make it devilish difficult to ascertain our doings."

Julian laid a hand on his chest, carefully, so as not to disturb the intricate folds of his neckcloth. "You misjudge me, my lady."

"I think not," the countess snapped. "Iddings, we shall take tea in the Blue Saloon. Betsy, change your gown and join us there at once."

"Yes, my lady," the butler replied, with a bow.

"Yes, Granmama," Betsy replied, with a curtsey.

Once the paneled mahogany doors of the adjacent Blue Saloon had closed behind her grandmother and Julian, Betsy spun on her heel to face Iddings and George. The butler and the footman had both come to her aid once this day. Fervently she hoped they would again.

"I should like to be shed of my upstart cousin as soon as possible," she told them. "Will you help me?"

Iddings and George glanced at each other, then

74

bowed in unison. "We would be honored, my lady," the butler replied.

"Thank you." Betsy gave them a grateful smile, then dropped to her heels to inquire of Boru, "And you, my darling?"

The hound whined and wiggled and licked her chin. Betsy hugged him, then rose to her feet, and said in a low voice to her conspirators, "This is what I want you to do . . ."

Chapter Eight

$\mathcal{T}$he Blue Saloon not only looked but smelled like the gardens at Clymore at their peak of fullest bloom. When Betsy made her entrance gowned in pink muslin trimmed with lace, the expression on Julian's face told her that he, too, was at his pique. Laughter bubbled in her throat at the pun, but she suppressed it as her cousin turned to face her.

"It would appear," he said, glancing ruefully at a towering arrangement of gladioli, "that you are something of a success."

"You seem surprised, my lord."

"I must own that I am."

"A gauche but honest confession," Betsy observed boldly, as she sat beside her grandmother on a striped satin settee. "As it happens, impetuousness and ramshackle behavior are all the rage just now."

"Amazing," Julian muttered, judging that the score of bouquets filling the saloon nearly equaled the number of dun letters he'd received from his creditors.

"How do you account for it, my lord? Do you suppose other members of the ton possess characters as flawed as my own? At our last meeting, you put forth the theory that such qualities are an unfortunate but natural outgrowth of being born to wealth and privilege. Do you still hold to that position? Or have you revised your opinion that such traits will ensure my failure in Society?"

Too late, as the upstart Earl of Clymore spun toward her, Lady Clymore trod on Betsy's foot. Anger glittered in his eyes, but Betsy held his gaze and her chin high.

Mistaking her impudence for defiance—when, in fact, it was nothing more than bravado born of her supreme confidence in Iddings and George—Julian further misjudged Betsy's plainspeaking to be as calculated as Lady Clymore's insistence that they take tea among these nauseatingly fragrant testimonies to her granddaughter's success. A careful orchestration, it appeared to him, designed to humiliate and belittle him.

He'd planned his visit intentionally early, hoping to find Betsy and the countess still at breakfast, which he would have had they kept town hours. He'd expected to be invited to join them, to be fawned and fussed over, to be greeted and treated with respect as the Earl of Clymore.

Instead, he'd been attacked and relegated to this mock orangery like the merest of social acquaintances. It was galling. He'd given his kinswomen ample time to adjust to his new status and accept their fate. That his own hinged on their wealth and marriage to Betsy was but another bitter pill, for he had no particular affection for his cousin.

And no time to woo another heiress. He'd been a fool, Julian realized, to let Lady Clymore wring the Christmas promise from him. An overconfident fool, which Betsy certainly was if she thought for an instant he would allow her to marry elsewhere. Her treatment of him made it clear that she still considered herself above his touch. If she would not grant him his due as the Earl of Clymore, Julian decided vengefully, then he would take it.

"Have you received anything other than flowers?" he asked, seating himself opposite Betsy on a matching settee.

"Some chocolates, a few sonnets," she replied modestly.

"You mistake my meaning. Deliberately, I think. Have you received any offers of marriage?"

"Such things," Lady Clymore responded tartly, "are not discussed in company."

"But we are family," Julian reminded her. "Somewhat distant, but family nonetheless. I merely wish to ascertain if I need to make myself available while in town to receive petitioners for Elizabeth's hand."

"You overstep yourself," the countess warned. "That duty is mine exclusively. I have your word, if you recall."

"I do, my lady, and assure you I have no intention of reneging." Julian laced his fingers together on his crossed knees. "But surely you see the problem?"

Lady Clymore glared down her nose at him, her eyes simmering. "I believe I am looking at it."

"Precisely." Julian nodded, well pleased with how easily the countess had taken his bait. "So long as I am in town, any gentleman who wishes to offer for Elizabeth will naturally seek me out as head of the family rather than yourself. It will be up to me to say yea or nay."

Lady Clymore paled. Julian smiled watching the

disdain fade from her eyes. Satisfied that at last he'd put the old termagant in her place, he glanced at Betsy, expecting to see a similarly shocked and glazed expression on her face. Instead, he saw the scorn his pronouncement had drained from her grandmother glittering coldly in her eyes.

"That is easily solved, Julian. You need only refer anyone who asks to Granmama."

"Surely you know I cannot."

"You mean you *will* not."

A knock at the saloon doors saved Julian from a reply. At Lady Clymore's acknowledgement, Iddings, shed of his apron and suitably rigged in his formal black coat, entered with the tea tray. As he placed it on the small table between the two settees, his gaze met Betsy's obliquely and inquiringly. She responded with a barely perceptible nod.

"That will be all." Lady Clymore dismissed the butler crisply, her composure recovered. "Betsy, you may pour."

She did so, noting that clever old Iddings had used the second-best tea service. Her grandmother seemed not to notice, so consumed was she with glaring daggers at Julian, who wouldn't know an outmoded china pattern if she broke every piece over his head. Which was an option, Betsy supposed, if all else failed.

But all else, in the form of Boru, had never failed her. The thought comforted Betsy—and enabled her to smile her prettiest smile as she handed Julian his cup and saucer.

"A compromise occurs to me," he said, addressing himself to the dowager as he leaned back to sip his tea, "a way by which we can both be at hand to receive any offers that may come Elizabeth's way."

"And what is that?" her ladyship inquired, as she raised her cup to her lips.

"I propose to take up residence here in Berkeley Square."

The outrageous suggestion caught Lady Clymore with a mouthful of tea half swallowed. Choking and spluttering, she snatched up her napkin, while Betsy whisked the cup and saucer out of her hand, hastily set it aside with her own on the table, and thumped her grandmother soundly on the back.

"Since we are family, no one of the ton will think it untoward," Julian finished, thinking dispassionately what a pity it would be if the old dragon strangled.

The old dragon did not, merely recovered her breath, her aplomb, and fixed a sulphurous gaze on the mushroom earl. The fiery setdown poised on her lips was forestalled, however, by another rap on the saloon doors.

"Come in and be quick about it!"

At Lady Clymore's scorchingly delivered admittance, Iddings nipped into the room, quickly announced, "Lord Theodore Earnshaw," then stepped aside with a bow. And a slight inclination of his head directed at Betsy.

Acknowledging the signal with a brief, upward lift of her chin, Betsy bowed her head but raised her eyes to watch Julian come to his feet as Teddy strode into the saloon. Nattily attired in a sable brown coat, russet waistcoat, buff pantaloons, and Hessians, he went first to her grandmother, as was proper, and bowed over the hand she lifted.

"How kind of you to call, Teddy," said Lady Clymore, banking her fire with obvious reluctance. "But I must own I was expecting Her Grace."

Displeasure narrowed Julian's gaze and thinned his mouth to a tight, white line. Betsy was unsure whether the cause was the familiarity of her grandmother's address, or the width of Teddy's unpadded shoulders, which masked the quick wink he gave her. Knowing Julian, she decided it was both.

"I bring her deepest apologies, my lady," Teddy replied, "and her promise to call upon you on the morrow."

"Her Grace is not indisposed, I trust?"

"Never, my lady." Teddy grinned as he straightened. "Merely at loose ends, for Lesley is to be wed next week."

"I've sent word that Betsy and I will attend. I trust Her Grace has received it?"

"I'm sure she has, my lady, but I will make it a point to tell her."

"Excellent." Lady Clymore's eyes began to smolder again as they settled on Julian. "Allow me to make you known to the Earl of Clymore, a most *distant* connection of my late husband's."

"Your servant, my lord." Teddy offered another bow and his hand.

Julian accepted it briefly. "A pleasure," he said, but the curt tone of his voice implied otherwise.

"Do please join us." Lady Clymore waved Teddy toward the settee occupied by Julian, as Iddings silently delivered another cup and saucer and withdrew. Leaving the saloon doors ajar behind him, Betsy noticed. "We were quite disappointed not to see you last evening at Lady Pinchon's rout."

"I was sorry to miss it, my lady, but I was otherwise engaged."

With his Latin grammar, Betsy surmised, for Teddy had confided his difficulties with that language to her when first they'd met at Lady Parkinson's ball. She'd volunteered to tutor him, which was the reason he had come, but she'd sooner dance with the Duke of Braxton again than admit the fact in front of Julian.

"Pity," the dowager said, turning a pointed look on her. "I believe Betsy saved a dance for you on her card. "Didn't you, m'dear?"

"Yes, Granmama," she replied, deftly following her grandmother's lead, "a waltz, just as you directed."

The embellishment was her own, added for its value to shock and aimed directly at Julian. It landed squarely on the mark, ellicting a curled-lip frown from her cousin, which Betsy took for an angry snarl.

In fact, it was a sneer of contempt. Did his kinswomen think him cloth-headed enough to believe this puppy was a serious rival? Obviously so, Julian decided, which was even more infuriating than their ridiculous efforts to bam him.

"If you will promise me another dance, Lady Elizabeth, I vow I will be there to partner you myself," Teddy said ardently to Betsy. "Though it was good of old Charles to stand up for me."

The sudden leap of Betsy's eyelids and the rush of color to her cheeks jolted Julian out of his glowering slouch. "Charles?" he queried sharply. "Charles who?"

"Why, my brother, of course," replied the puppy, eyeing Julian as if he'd just come to town in the back of a farm wagon. "The Duke of Braxton."

Julian gaped, first at Teddy, then at Betsy, who was nearly as stunned as her cousin. How did Teddy know the duke had danced with her? She assumed his brother had told him, but what if, instead, one of Lady Pinchon's guests had come unseen into the foyer? Deaf and blind as they had all appeared to be, there was, Betsy knew, no surer cure for failing sensibilities among the ton than a whiff of scandal.

But questioning Teddy at length must wait, for there was a mushroom to be rid of, and so she said, "It was most kind of His Grace to lead me out," and lowered her gaze.

Not to appear missish—though if Julian so misread it all the better—but to hide the guilt she feared might show on her face at telling such a blatant lie. This was, Betsy realized uncomfortably, the third she'd told since breakfast. Prevarication was not in her nature, at least it had not been so until she'd come to London.

Telling herself she'd done no more in the present instance than dance to the tune first struck by her grandmother and then by Teddy was small comfort. The fact remained that the half-truths she'd begun upon her arrival in town had ballooned into complete fabrications. Which caused her gaze to lift to Julian, still staring at her slack-jawed and thunderstruck, and quelled the impulse she felt to confess.

Desperate circumstances called for desperate measures. She was not the one who'd dumped the Duke of Braxton into this particular bag of moonshine; Teddy had done that, but if she could tie the strings of it about his head for the sake of leading Julian to believe she was on the verge of receiving an offer, then so be it. Such a small favor was the very least His Grace owed her for ruining her gown and her evening. But not her reputation, she hoped, for the moment pushing that worry aside.

"Charles quite enjoyed himself," Teddy went on, lying blithely with a skill that amazed Betsy. "He said to tell you so, and asked if you would grant him another waltz at the Countess Featherston's ball tomorrow evening."

"I—would be delighted," Betsy replied, hoping Julian would take the halt in her voice for maidenly demure.

It was, in fact, incredulity, for the knot newly tied in an already twisted skein would serve no purpose other than to assure Julian's presence at the Countess Featherston's ball. How Teddy imagined that would help her cause she hadn't a clue, but trusted the speaking look he gave her signified a method to his madness.

"Will Her Grace not object?" Julian asked.

"My mother?" Teddy regarded him with a dubiously arched eyebrow. "I should think not, my lord."

The misconstruction Julian had made was quite natural, but the look of naked fury that contorted his features as Teddy corrected him was not. It should have frightened her, Betsy supposed, since it was focused solely upon her, but it did not. Rather it exulted her, for it was the first clear indication of a breach in the Earl of Clymore's wall of overweening arrogance.

"Really, Julian," Lady Clymore sniffed. "Everyone who is anyone knows that Braxton is unwed, and that the duchess is a dowager. I advise you do a bit of boning up lest you make a complete cake of yourself in Society."

"I shall do so, my lady. You may count upon it." The earl banged his cup and saucer down on the tea service and rose. "Now if you will excuse me."

He bowed first to Lady Clymore, then Betsy, accorded Teddy a barely civil nod, and strode to the saloon doors.

Catching the one Iddings had left ajar by the knob, Julian swung abruptly back to glare at them. "You may *all* count upon it," he repeated, the fury in his gaze deepening his voice with ominous undertones.

He swung the door wide then to stalk through it, but before he could take a step, Boru lunged past him into the saloon. Stunned and openmouthed, Julian watched the hound gather himself to leap at the settee, then nearly fell over his own feet in his haste to escape the saloon and slam the door behind him.

"Boru, no!" Betsy sprang to her feet, but too late, for the hound was already launching himself into the air.

Wide-eyed with horror at the shaggy missile hurtling toward him, Teddy could do nothing but fling up his arms as the hound landed on the striped satin cushions. Lady Clymore shrieked, so did Teddy, and Betsy clapped her hands over her eyes as the settee went crashing over backward.

Chapter Nine

Fervently praying Teddy was unhurt, or if he was that the Duke of Braxton's country seat did not contain a dungeon, Betsy swept her hands away from her eyes and rushed across the saloon. Holding her breath, she peered over the edge of the upended settee, her heart nearly stopping when she saw Teddy.

He was sprawled on his back, Boru straddling his chest. The hound's mouth was open, but his teeth were not clamped around Teddy's throat as it first appeared. Nor was Teddy holding Boru off by the scruff of his neck. He was merely scratching his ears.

"What a fine fellow you are," he said admiringly.

Betsy nearly swooned with relief and pressed one hand to her throat. "Are you all right?"

"Perfectly." Teddy glanced up at her and grinned. "What a whacking great dog. Is he yours?"

The saloon doors burst open then, spilling an eager Iddings and George into the room. "Did Boru get 'im, m'lady?" The footman asked. Iddings gave him a sharp look and an even sharper elbow in the ribs.

"Lend a hand, quickly," Betsy said, avoiding her grandmother's suspiciously narrowed gaze as she rounded the settee to catch Boru's collar and tug him off Teddy.

She drew the hound aside, while George righted the settee, and Iddings helped Teddy to his feet. Once the rug had been straightened and the tails of Teddy's coat brushed, the footman and the butler made for the door.

"I have not given you leave to go," Lady Clymore said, her imperious tone turning the servants in their tracks to face her. "Am I to understand that it was by design rather than accident that Boru found his way into this room?"

"It was, Granmama," Betsy confessed. "The plan was to be rid of Julian and it was exclusively mine. Iddings and George are blameless. I impressed them."

"Is this true?" the dowager demanded of her majordomo.

"Beg pardon, Lady Elizabeth." Iddings made a small bow in her direction. "But it is my recollection that we volunteered."

"Mine as well, m'lady," George agreed staunchly.

"They are merely trying to protect me, Granmama," Betsy countered. "The fault is mine entirely."

"I do not doubt that," Lady Clymore retorted, fixing a fierce gaze on her servants. Her scathing tone made Betsy cringe, and George and Iddings stiffen. "Given the serious nature of this misdeed, I have no choice but to sentence you both to an extra half day. That is all. You may go."

"Yes, my lady," they murmured in unison, bowing quickly to hide their startled but appreciative grins.

"Iddings." The countess turned the butler about

as he and George reached the doorway. "If it should in future be necessary to implement such a plan, I suggest you listen at the door to make sure Boru pounces on the *right* quarry."

"I shall, my lady," he promised, with a twinkle in his eye, then followed George from the room and shut the doors.

"Punish me if you must," Betsy said as her grandmother wheeled toward her, "but spare Boru. He is guilty only of despising Julian."

"As do we all." Lady Clymore gingerly reached out her hand to pat the top of Boru's head. He cringed at her touch, but when she did not rap him with her knuckles, he lifted his ears and thumped his tail against the floor. "Had you confided your plan to me, I would have tripped Julian on his way to the door."

"I would give passing marks in Latin to see that," Teddy said, with a laugh.

"You need wager nothing, only call upon the morrow," Betsy told him unhappily, "for unless we can persuade him otherwise, Julian intends to take up residence with us."

"Persuasion will not be necessary," Lady Clymore replied firmly. "This house is mine, entailed to me by my mother. He has no claim here, and I shall tell him so when next he calls. Hopefully with his trunks in hand—so that I may have the pleasure of casting him bag and baggage into the street!"

"So it is!" A smile lit Betsy's face, but only for a moment. "And what of the ton? Will Julian not bruit it about that you refused him hospitality?"

"Let him." The dowager sniffed and took herself back to the settee. "An evening or two in the company of the Earl of Clymore will give Society the right of it, I think."

Just as another dance or two with the lovely Lady Elizabeth, Teddy thought, would further persuade Charles of their suitability. That his brother was at least partially convinced he had no doubt, for the duke had come home very late the night before. Without his coat and in a towering rage.

The memory of Charles slamming into the Bond Street house shouting for brandy brought a smile to Teddy's face, for it signified that the first stumbling block to his plan had been overcome—His Majesty's Ship Braxton was no longer becalmed. Now its youthful but well-seasoned captain had only to steer a course into the heart of the golden-haired tempest, who was presently seating herself next to her grandmother on the settee.

"Most assuredly, Lady Clymore," Teddy said, cheerfully agreeing with the countess. "Just as *seeing* Lady Betsy dance with a duke will make a much greater impression upon his lordship than merely hearing me tell of it."

"It will make an even larger impression on His Grace," Betsy threatened, her temper and the memory of her humiliation at the hands of the Duke of Braxton overriding discretion. "An impression the size of my reticule, which I will most assuredly put in his head if he so much as *dares* to come near me."

Again Lady Clymore trod upon her toes. But this time Betsy trod back.

"Ouch!" her ladyship squawked, more from surprise than pain. "That's my gouty foot, you wretched gel!"

"Fustian," Betsy said, turning her attention to

Teddy. "How do you know His Grace stood up with me?"

Tiny sparks gleamed in her deep blue eyes. If he fed them a bit of fuel, Teddy thought, perhaps he could goad Betsy into telling him what happened at Lady Pinchon's rout to set her and Charles at odds.

"Why, he told me, of course."

The spark dimmed a bit, with relief, Teddy guessed, but her gaze narrowed a fraction. "Did he say anything else?"

"He mentioned that he loaned you his coat."

The spark flared, almost but not quite burst into flame. "Did he say why?"

"I believe he said you took a chill while walking in the garden."

"*What?*" Lady Clymore shrieked, leaping from the settee firmly onto her gouty foot. "I shall call him out!"

"Sit down, Granmama." Betsy's voice was cool, but her eyes were not. They never wavered from Teddy's face, and flickered vividly with sapphire flame. "I went nowhere near the garden with His Grace. I merely threatened to slap him for even suggesting it."

"That is sufficient grounds for a challenge!" Lady Clymore declared, fumbling beneath her shawl for the pockets of her morning gown. "A glove! I shall need a glove! And a second—"

"Granmama, *sit*." Tearing her gaze from Teddy, Betsy grasped her ladyship's wrist and tugged her down on the settee. "As it happens, His Grace said nothing about the garden. He said *pardon*, which I mistook for *garden*."

"He did? *Oh!* Well then," Lady Clymore blustered huffily. "Loud as the demmed music was I don't wonder. My head is still ringing from it."

" 'Twas not just the music, Granmama. I stuffed lamb's wool in my ears."

"Lamb's wool!" her ladyship squawked. "Wretched gel! Did you not think to share it with me?"

"I also mistook His Grace to say *bother* when he said *brother*," Betsy said, her gaze swinging back to Teddy, slitted and smoldering with suspicion.

"Well, of course he did; you told me that! 'Twas the reason he came, you said, to make you cry off from—" Lady Clymore broke off her tirade and turned her head to add her fearsome glare to the one Betsy had trained upon Teddy. "*You* put the idea in his head, didn't you, you scamp?"

"I must own that I did, my lady," Teddy confessed.

"How *could* you?"

The tears in Betsy's eyes gleamed more with hurt than fury. Boru sidled around the corner of the settee, laid his head in her lap, and rolled mournful brown eyes at Teddy.

Lady Clymore rose purposefully. "Give me your glove, you ungrateful, perfidious pup."

"I ask only a chance to explain myself," Teddy replied, getting quickly to his feet. "If my reasons do not suit my lady I will name my seconds."

Betsy and her grandmother exchanged a look, then the countess sat down. "We are listening," she said coldly.

"I beg you recall his lordship's reaction when I told him Lady Betsy danced last night with a duke. Not just any duke, but an *unwed* duke."

Betsy flushed guiltily, for the advantage in leading Julian to think she'd attracted the attention of a peer of greater rank had already selfishly occurred to her. "Of course we recall it, and our own shameful part in furthering the notion that His Grace stood up with me for purely social reasons, but that hardly excuses you—"

"Certainly it does not," Teddy cut in. "I most deeply regret that I was unable to apprise you of what I had done, but Charles locked me in my room with my valet and my Latin grammar last evening. I could not even send you a note."

"Knows you well, doesn't he?" Lady Clymore observed.

"Indeed he does, my lady." Teddy grinned unabashedly. "It struck me upon first hearing of Lady Betsy's plight that the interest of a duke would be the very thing to keep her cousin at bay until she can make an equitable match."

Betsy's eyes widened with alarm. "Surely you did *not* suggest such a thing to His Grace!"

"Of course not," Teddy assured her. "I merely led him to believe that you and I were on the verge of eloping to Gretna Green."

Lady Clymore made a noise in her throat that was more moan than groan, clapped a hand over her eyes, and fell heavily back against the cushions of the settee.

"You what?" Betsy gaped at Teddy, the color draining from her face.

"I could hardly tell Charles the truth," he replied logically, "and ask him to pretend interest in you."

"Why ever not?" The countess demanded, lowering her hand from her face just as a knock sounded at the saloon doors. "Yes, Iddings. What is it?"

"My lady," he said, stepping into the room. "The Earl of Clymore has taken himself no farther than the flagway outside the gates."

"What the devil is he doing there?"

"It would appear that he is turning away visitors."

"*What?*" Betsy shrieked along with her grandmother, following on the dowager's heels—as Teddy and Boru followed on hers—when Lady Clymore leapt from the settee and rushed into the foyer behind Iddings.

A frown on his face and a spying glass in his hand, George stood at one of the tall windows fronting the courtyard. He stepped aside, drawing the velvet drapery with him to give Lady Clymore, Betsy, and Teddy a better view.

Laying a hand on Boru's head as he wiggled between them, Betsy looked across the courtyard and through the iron spikes of the fence at Julian, strolling up and down the flagway. A discreet distance away, a hired hackney waited, the driver lounging in his box. A growl rumbled in Boru's throat, but Betsy soothed him by scratching his ears as a carriage swung into the square and stopped before the house.

By the time the coachman placed the steps and opened the door, Julian was there to greet the occupant. Betsy watched them shake hands, saw her cousin stretch an arm across the gentleman's shoulders and draw him away from the gates.

"Who is that?" Lady Clymore demanded, all but pressing her nose to the glass as well. "I cannot quite make out his features."

" 'Tis difficult to tell at this distance." Teddy

stood on tiptoe and craned his neck. "But it may be the Marquess of Claxton."

The name, at least, was familiar to Betsy. She'd last seen it earlier that morning—penned in a horrible hand at the bottom of the most dreadful poem she'd ever read.

" 'Ere, m'lord." George offered his spying glass. "Kep' this when I left the docks."

"Good fellow." Teddy opened the glass and squinted into the eyepiece. "It is Claxton. And look! He is returning to his carriage."

"Let me see." Betsy claimed the glass and raised it in time to see the marquess clap Julian on the shoulder in a congratulatory fashion before remounting the steps and disappearing inside his carriage.

"Give me that." Lady Clymore snatched the glass, but Betsy did not need it to see the triumphant grin that spread across her cousin's face when the coach rolled away out of the square. "Come back, you clunch!" the countess shrieked furiously.

Betsy shot a simmering glare at Teddy. "What do you make of this?"

"I would guess," he replied grimly, "that his lordship has persuaded Claxton that his time is wasted here."

"Snake," Betsy hissed murderously as she swung back to the window and watched Julian resume his apparently casual stroll around the square. It was one thing to scheme herself free of unwanted suitors, but quite another for her cousin to do so.

"I shall summon the watch!" Lady Clymore declared.

"To what end, my lady?" Teddy countered. " 'Tis

a public street and his lordship is an earl. He can further claim acquaintance with you to explain his presence."

"I will not allow that despicable upstart to chase off Betsy's suitors!" With a loud *thwack*, Lady Clymore collapsed the spying glass between her hands. "I will shoot him and say I mistook him for a cut purse. Anyone who knows Dameron will not doubt me. Iddings! The dueling pistols!"

"Wait, Granmama." Betsy turned toward her, a devilish gleam in her eyes. "Isn't it time for Boru's exercise?"

At the mention of his name, the hound turned his head from the window, whined, and wagged his tail.

"Why, yes." Lady Clymore smiled with fiendish glee. "I believe it is."

"I'll fetch his lead," George said, darting away toward the kitchen.

"Soames! My pelisse!" Betsy shouted for her abigail, hiked her skirts, and raced for the stairs, her lacy petticoat frothing about her ankles as she sprang up them two at a time.

"I'll get my hat." Grinning, Teddy rubbed his hands together and crossed to the hall table to collect it.

"Let's leave nothing to chance." Lady Clymore nodded sagely to Iddings. "Bring the pistols."

Chapter Ten

The butler returned from the game room with a pair of silver-inlaid Forsyth pistols in a mahogany case just as Betsy came pelting downstairs in a pink pelisse and bonnet that matched her gown, and George came back with Boru's lead. Once the hound was securely leashed, Iddings opened the door, and Betsy took Teddy's arm.

With her reticule looped over her elbow, she went first down the steps, at the bottom tugging Teddy aside to let Boru and George pass. Eagerly the hound towed the footman across the chilly, sun-splashed courtyard, where young Lord Earnshaw's groom and dark green curricle waited.

"Be sure you shoo him this way!" Lady Clymore called.

"Don't even think it," Betsy warned Teddy. "She might actually shoot him."

Lifting one hand to her bonnet, she rounded the gatepost behind George and Boru in time to see Julian, some few yards ahead on the flagway, raise his cane to the brown-haired urchin boy and his little dog.

"Stop!" she cried, breaking into a run as Julian's cane came down.

The boy dodged the blow and dove for the gutter,

the terrier yelped, and Boru let out a howl. As he raised his cane again, Julian shot a glare over his shoulder, his jaw dropping at the sight of the huge hound dragging a sprawled George behind him as he lunged past Betsy. The footman clung desperately to the lead, but his weight was too great. The leather snapped, freeing Boru to the hunt with a second joyful howl. Grabbing his hat, Julian bolted for the hackney waiting near the mouth of the square.

"Boru! Come back!" Betsy skidded to a halt, bit off her glove, and stuck her fingers in the corners of her mouth.

The long, piercing whistle she gave had no effect. Baying his bloodcurdling wolf's cry, Boru ran at full stride in pursuit of his quarry.

"I'll get 'im, m'lady." George pushed himself off the pavement and went racing after the hound.

Praying the footman would catch him, Betsy rushed toward the boy, with Teddy a step or two behind her. Arms wrapped protectively around his dog, he huddled in a pile of leaves blown into the gutter. He threw back his head when Betsy fell on her knees beside him and gripped his shoulders, his eyes blue and huge in his pale, pinched face. First with fear at the sight of Teddy, then with wonder and recognition when Betsy smoothed her ungloved hand over his dirty forehead and ragged hair.

"Are you hurt?" she asked.

"N-no, m'lady."

"And Scraps?"

" 'E's all right. Just skeered."

The crack of a pistol made Betsy jerk her head around to see her grandmother on the steps of the house, the Forsyth pistol gripped in her hand, smoking and pointed skyward. She swung back then and saw Julian, no more than five steps ahead of Boru, fling open the hackney door and dive inside.

When a second shot rang out, the horses reared in their traces, the jolt slapping the door shut in Boru's face. With a furious howl, he leapt up the side of the coach in a vain attempt to reach Julian. The driver did his best, but by now his horses were beyond control. As soon as their front hooves touched ground they bolted, lurching the hackney away from the gutter and across the square.

"Boru, no!" Betsy shouted, pulling the boy with her as she scrambled to her feet. "Boru, stop!"

She whistled again, but futilely, for Boru was beyond hearing. Clutching the boy and the squirming, yapping terrier in his arms to her skirts, she watched helplessly as the hackney careened out of Berkeley Square onto Davies Street with Boru howling and nipping at the rear wheels and George running valiantly behind.

Even when safely ensconced in a sturdy, well-sprung coach, the streets of London were dangerous. For an overzealous wolfhound intent only on running his quarry to ground they were certain peril.

"If Boru suffers so much as a scratch, I will shoot Julian myself!" Betsy threatened, clenching her hands into fists and drawing the boy closer.

"Come along, quickly." Teddy closed an urgent hand on her elbow. "We'll follow in my curricle."

"Me an' Scraps'll point the way." Wriggling free of Betsy, the boy put his dog down and wrapped the string around his wrist. " 'Urry up, mister!"

His rags flying around him, the boy dashed away. Scraps ran alongside, barking and limping only a little. Wheeling about and gesturing with one arm, Teddy shouted at his groom to bring his curricle.

Betsy murmured prayers and stifled tears. She hadn't reckoned on the boy and his dog appearing, Julian's cruelty—though she'd long suspected her cousin possessed such a streak—or Boru's reaction to it. Nonetheless, if anything happened to her darling, the blame could be laid on her dish. Even so, she would shoot Julian.

In a clatter of hooves the curricle arrived, drawn by a pair of gleaming blacks. The tiger jumped off before the wheels stopped turning, handed Betsy up onto the dark green leather seat, then passed the leads to his young master and stood clear as Teddy vaulted into the curricle.

With a single flick of the ribbons they were off, a spiral of red-gold leaves swirling up from the gutter in their wake. They reached Davies Street, a straight shot out of Berkeley Square, with Teddy leaning to his left to spy the boy, and Betsy, her cheeks flushed by the rush of the cool autumn wind, bobbing and craning beside him to do the same.

"There!" She pointed at a small, ragged figure jumping up and down and waving madly on the corner just ahead.

"Hyah!" Teddy shouted, urging his blacks to greater speed, as the boy and Scraps sprang away onto Brook Street, headed toward Grosvenor Square.

The curricle followed, making the turn very nearly under the noses of a bay draft team drawing a heavily loaded dray. Teddy lost his hat in the process, and Betsy her bonnet when she looked back to see the bays clopping placidly past the corner as if they hadn't just missed a collision by inches.

Her bonnet bouncing against her shoulders by the strings tied around her throat, Betsy bit her lip in consternation as the blacks plunged out of Brook Street into Grosvenor Square. Neither the boy and his dog nor the hackney were anywhere to be seen.

"Oh, where *are* they?" she asked worriedly, twisting about on the seat.

"They didn't double back or we'd have run smack into them," Teddy said, thinking out loud as he pulled back on the leathers. "If they kept straight to Upper Brook Street they'll end at—"

"Park Lane!" Betsy gasped, her thoughts jumping ahead of his.

"Good God!" Teddy blanched and snatched up his whip.

With a flick of his wrist he cracked it above the heads of his horses. Their ears sprang forward and they leapt ahead, the houses of the haut ton flashing by in a blur.

Paralleling Hyde Park, Park Lane was one of the busiest, ergo the most lethal, thoroughfares in all of London. Picturing Boru running amok into its midst in pursuit of the hackney brought tears to Betsy's eyes.

Heavier traffic on Upper Brook Street made speed impossible. The blacks chafed when Teddy drew them in and so did Betsy. She strained to look ahead for a glimpse of the boy and saw him, near the juncture of Upper Brook Street and Park Lane. She also saw an overturned farm wagon, its load of turnips spilled on the pavement, and a shiny red barouch halfway up on the flagway with a broken wheel, and groaned.

"I believe we're on the right track," Teddy said

needlessly, as he deftly steered the curricle around the wrecks.

The boy stood on the corner, jumping and pointing toward the orange and gold canopy of trees within Hyde Park. Betsy lifted a hand to acknowledge him, then shrieked as he sprang without looking off the flagway into Park Lane. Squeezing her eyes shut, she waited for the shouts of coachmen and the screams of horses that never came.

"Oh, no," she moaned, opening her eyes to utter chaos as Teddy steered the blacks through the turn onto Park Lane.

A clear path stretched from Upper Brook Street to the Grosvenor Gate leading into the park, for the edges of the road were lined with carriages, drays, wagons, and curricles. All had come to rest at odd, abrupt angles, as if they'd been swept into the gutter by a great wind.

Or a whacking great dog.

The boy was hopping up and down and waving both arms before the gate. He pointed into the park, then took a firm hold on the string tied to Scraps, and ducked away into the crowds of onlookers on the flagway.

"Come back!" Betsy shouted, uselessly, for he'd already melted away into the throng.

"He daren't enter the park," Teddy told her, as he slowed the blacks to make the turn.

Betsy knew it was so, but nonetheless despised a society that begrudged a poor and hungry child a glimpse of green. Twice he'd come to the house in Berkeley Square. With luck, he would come again, and when he did, she would do what she could for him. The vow made, Betsy turned her gaze forward in search of Boru as the curricle swept past the gates.

There was no sign of him, the hackney, or of George. Only drably dressed nannies with prams and chubby toddlers in tow, a few couples strolling, and one or two horsemen. None of them seemed particularly overset, which suggested to Betsy that Boru had not come this way. At least not yet.

Easing his team to a walk, Teddy made a quick survey of the area, his gaze locking on a lone gentleman some distance away on a leaf-scattered stretch of green to the left of the path. Hatless and shed of his coat, he was flying a pair of monstrous yellow kites with bright-colored rags tied to their tails.

"If I didn't know better, I'd swear that was—"

"Boru!" Betsy cried joyfully, interrupting Teddy as the hound came bounding around a sharp curve in the path just ahead and she sprang toward the side of the curricle.

Boru was in hot pursuit of a rabbit, and George was in hot pursuit of him. The footman's face was nearly purple—and he was beginning to stumble with exhaustion.

The blacks snorted and laid back their ears, which drove all thoughts of the man with the kites from Teddy's head. If he hadn't snatched the bits from his team with a dab-handed tug on the leathers, they might have bolted at Betsy's sudden lurch. He held them steady as she jumped to the ground, then set the brake, looped the leads over it, and bailed out of the curricle.

Hiking her dress and pelisse nearly to her knees, Betsy ran like a deer behind Boru as the rabbit dodged left off the path onto the grass. A moment before he stumbled into them headfirst, Teddy leapt in front of his team and caught George as the footman nearly swooned and fell into his arms.

"Where is his lordship?" Teddy demanded.

"L-long g-gone, m'lord," George panted. "Nearly h-had 'im we did, then the beast spied hisself a r-rabbit an' we 'us off agin t'other direction."

"Well done." Teddy let him go and stepped back. "You may rest now."

"Thank you, m'lord." George's eyes rolled back in his head and he collapsed safely out of reach of the blacks' teeth.

The rabbit was not so lucky, Teddy saw, as he wheeled off the path at a run. Only a desperate last-second leap saved the summer-fattened hare from Boru's snapping jaws. It was a less than graceful lunge, which sent the hound skidding along the leaf-strewn grass on his chin. And Betsy behind him on her stomach as she made a grab for the hound that missed when he found his feet again and went charging off after his quarry.

"Blister it, Boru! Come back here!" Betsy sprang up on her knees, snatching leaves from her hair and flinging her bonnet, which now rested beneath her chin, over her shoulder. As she did so, the heavy reticule looped over her elbow swung in a wide arc and nearly toppled her again.

Tripping over her torn pelisse and gown, she struggled to her feet. Teddy reached her side and caught her arm, which gave her the moment of balance she needed to tug her reticule over her elbow, kick her skirts out of her way, and gather them up again.

Mere inches ahead of Boru, the rabbit bounded across the green. Projecting its leaping, zigzag course, Teddy realized the man with the kites, whose back was turned to the pursuit, stood squarely in the rabbit's path. The hare could be trusted to veer off in time, but what of Boru?

"Oh, Teddy! That gentleman!" Betsy gasped, her eyes widening as the same thought struck her. "Sir! Sir!" she called, pulling Teddy to a halt so she could shout louder.

"You there!" he yelled, cupping his hands around his mouth.

It was no use. The brisk wind that held the kites aloft tossed and rattled the autumn-dry trees dotting the lawn and muffled their shouts. Just as Teddy had predicted, the rabbit leapt nimbly aside at the last possible moment—but Boru did not. He crashed into the man with the force of a runaway carriage, upending the poor devil and spinning him around in a midair tangle of strings.

The kites plummeted earthward, their twisted tails engulfing Boru. Horror engulfed Teddy as he watched man and hound, hopelessly entwined in strings and rag-tied tails, tumble to the ground.

The poor devil was his brother Charles.

Chapter Eleven

*O*h, God, let this be a nightmare, Betsy prayed, clapping one hand over her eyes and clutching Teddy's sleeve in the other. Let me waken in my bed in my night rail. Let me open my eyes and see anyone but the Duke of Braxton.

Unfortunately he was still there, sprawled and unmoving on the turf beneath Boru when she spread her fingers and peeked between them. "Oh, *no*," she moaned. "Not *again*."

"What do you mean, 'not again'?" Teddy demanded, prying her fingers from his arm and spinning sharply toward her.

"I mean," Betsy explained, her voice little more than a dismal groan, "that I first made your brother's acquaintance when our carriages stopped side by side in Oxford Street. I tore the sleeve of his coat, and Boru knocked him senseless."

"My apologies, Lady Betsy," Teddy said, as he grabbed her hand and pulled her into a run, "but damn and blast it!"

Stumbling along behind him, Betsy wished desperately she could be anywhere—or *anyone*—else. Netted by strings like a giant furry fish, Boru turned his head as she approached and whined imploringly. Charles lay spread-eagled in a tangle of kite tails beneath him, a grass stain smeared from cheek to chin, eyes closed but his lashes fluttering.

Sinking next to him in a billow of ruined skirts, Betsy placed one hand on Boru to soothe the trembling hound, lifted the other to smooth Charles's tousled hair from his forehead, and froze. Where had the impulse to touch him come from? Surely it was only concern for his well-being, not the sudden and vibrantly remembered sweep of his arm about her waist the night before. Or perhaps it was simple light-headedness. Caused by exertion, Betsy told herself firmly, not the vivid recollection of the torchlight flickering across his handsome features.

"This is hopeless." Teddy grimly surveyed the latticework of kite tails ensnaring Charles and Boru, then rocked back on his heels to pat the pockets of his waistcoat. "We'll have to cut them loose."

"You can't mean with *that*!" Betsy exclaimed, incredulously, at the penknife he produced. "It will take all day!"

"Have you a better idea? Or perhaps another knife in your bag of tricks?"

"As it happens, I do." Betsy flung her reticule off her arm, thrust her hands indignantly on her hips, and glared at Teddy. "And allow me to point out, Lord Earnshaw, that if I were a man, I wouldn't have to resort to a *bag of tricks*!"

"This is no time to be on your high ropes." Teddy shot her a frown as he caught a handful of strings and began cutting them. "I do not stand especially high in Charles's esteem at the moment, and judging by the tale you've just told me—and the way he stormed into our mother's house last night— neither, my lady, do *you*."

" 'Stormed'?" Betsy repeated faintly, her eyes widening.

"Yes, *stormed*." Teddy clipped the last of the string he held and gathered up another handful. "In a towering rage and shouting for brandy."

Memory and dread laced a chill up Betsy's back as she recalled Charles glaring at her across Lady Pinchon's ballroom, the flash of breaking glass as he'd snapped his goblet cleanly in half. "Quickly, keep cutting," she told Teddy, as she jerked open her reticule and began pawing through it. "I have Papa's knife in here *somewhere*."

She could have the crown jewels as well, Teddy thought darkly, as the pair of spectacles she'd shown him at Lady Parkinson's plopped into her lap. Wisely, however, he did not say so, simply watched a snuffbox roll off her knee and a purse heavy with coins jingle onto Charles's chest.

When a set of hazard dice rolled across the torn and muddied hem of her gown, Teddy grinned. When a volume of Ovid's *Amores* bounced open on its cover, its pages ruffling in the breeze, he sat back hard on his heels.

The scandalous Roman work was the only book written in Latin, poetry or prose, that he'd ever managed to stumble through on his own. Avidly, with a rapidly thudding pulse, by the faint light of a single candle in a dark, secret stairway at his school in the Midlands.

"Capital choice!" he exclaimed, his meaning escaping Betsy until she looked up and saw the fallen volume and Teddy's eager expression.

"Our study of Latin will be confined to Caesar's legions and the parts of Gaul," she said scathingly, flushing as she snatched up the book and laid it aside. "*Not* the anatomical parts of the ladies of the Roman court."

"My deepest apologies," Teddy said, his face scalding, "but I thought—"

"I know *precisely* what you thought." At last, Betsy's hand closed on the hilt of her father's knife. She withdrew it slowly from its sheath, watching with satisfaction the incredulous leap of Teddy's eyelids. "But I keep Ovid in my reticule only as a last resort."

"Gemini!" Teddy swallowed hard. "I should think *that* would make a much better last resort."

That was no mere penknife. It was a dagger, with a jewel-crusted hilt and wickedly keen blade.

A stiff gust of wind rustled the nearby trees where one of Charles's kites had come to rest. A shaft of sunlight sliced through the torn yellow paper stretched across the frame, gleamed on the finely honed blade, and, just as Charles's eyelids slowly fluttered open, caught and blazed like a diamond on the viciously pointed tip.

Blinded by the glare, Charles winced and blinked to clear the dazzle and the tears it brought from his eyes. When he opened them again, his wet lashes made a halo of the sunlight shimmering on Betsy's golden hair and a misty blur of her elegant profile. His dulled senses and befuddled mind told him this was no earthly vision.

He dimly recalled coming to the park to launch the kites he'd constructed to carry his wind device aloft for further testing, remembered being lifted off his feet, but nothing else. He'd obviously fallen, but where? Such ethereally beautiful creatures as the one before him did not frequent Hyde Park.

Heaven mayhap, or Mount Olympus. Was she an angel, or was she perhaps—

"Bloody hell!" Charles shouted, as his vision finally cleared and he recognized the face before him. "*You* again!"

Unaware of the kite tails entwining his limbs, he shot straight up on his spine, and from there halfway to his knees, the sudden stress on the strings threatening to yank Boru off his feet. Yelping and scrabbling madly, the hound did his best to keep his balance, but his strength was no match for the inexorable pull on the web of strings binding him to Charles. Several snapped under the strain, but the rest held, flinging him like a missile from a sling into the chest of the Duke of Braxton.

"Bloody *damned* hell!" Charles howled with rage, as he realized—too late—his predicament and threw up his arms to ward off the worst of the impact.

To Betsy, his upflung hands signaled an intent to throttle Boru. "Unhand my darling, you beast!" she cried, dropping the dagger and leaping at Boru as he and Charles went crashing to the ground in a splash of vivid leaves.

By a scant inch at best, Teddy managed to scramble free of the melee and scoop up the dagger. Springing to his feet, he hopped left and right and back and forth, nipping into the fracas to cut strings whenever a safe opening presented itself. But Charles thrashed one way, Betsy kicked another, and Boru lunged a third, which only further twisted and tangled the strings.

"Damn your eyes, Chas; *hold still!*" Teddy bellowed, but to no avail, for the thrashing and kicking continued.

Intending to fetch his whip and crack it over their

heads to get their attention, Teddy buried the dagger safely to its hilt in the leafy ground. He wheeled around, already running, in time to see a yellow phaeton bearing Lady Clymore, and Charles's coach with Fletcher at the ribbons, converging from opposite directions on the spot where his curricle stood and George was scraping himself to his feet.

"Huzzah! Reinforcements!" Teddy whooped, and sprinted toward them.

Charles only half heard his brother's shout, yet didn't dare turn away from the golden-haired hoyden roundly pummeling him to see what was afoot now. The ringing in his ears, the blood pounding madly through his veins, and the brief glimpse he'd had of the dagger convinced him in his addled state that Betsy meant to kill him for thwarting her schemes with Teddy.

The little Delilah! To think he'd envied her flock of beaux the night before, that he'd ached to be one of them, that he had, God help him, felt his chest swell with pride when he'd led her onto the dance floor. To think, just now, at first regaining his senses, he'd thought her more lovely than Aphrodite.

Spurred by rage and the splitting pain in his head, Charles trapped her wrists in his hands. "What is your plan now, my lady? Since you failed to cut my throat, do you intend to beat me to death with your tiny little fists?"

"If you so much as lay a finger on my darling," Betsy threatened breathlessly, in her fury totally oblivious to the fact that she was perched most shockingly upon him, "I will, so help me!"

"So he's your darling now, is he?"

"He has been since he was but a pup!"

"Silly chit! He *is* a pup!"

"No more than my fists are tiny!" Betsy wrenched her right wrist free and landed a solid punch on Charles's chin that snapped his head back.

The follow through left her sprawled across his chest, knuckles throbbing, eyes wide with horror as she realized she'd just struck a peer of the realm. Never mind that he deserved the facer for his high-handed treatment of her, he was still a duke, and she was supposed to be a lady.

"Your Grace, forgive me!" Betsy pushed her hands against his shoulders and shot up into a sitting position. "I can't think what came over me!"

Charles could, remembering now the streak of menace he'd first observed in her nature in Oxford Street, but he was unable to say so. The best he could manage was a dazed and groaning, "Ungh," as he raised a hand and gingerly worked his stinging jaw.

The lift of his arm and a well-timed lunge by Boru applied sufficient stress on the kite strings to break them at last with an audible *pling*. Released from his confinement, the hound shot like a rocket past Teddy, tail tucked between his legs and howling, the close brush of his flank nearly spinning young Lord Earnshaw off his feet.

Flinging a look over her shoulder, Betsy saw Boru streak toward the carriages just drawing to a halt on the verge, the bits of frayed string snagged in his coat streaming behind him like flags. She saw Teddy pinwheeling his arms to keep his balance, George stumbling away from the curricle to intercept Boru, and scrambled hastily to her feet. Sticking the ungloved fingers of her right hand in her mouth, she sucked a deep breath and whistled.

"Ungh," Charles groaned again, clapping both hands over his ears to muffle the piercing shrill that cut like a knife through his madly ringing head.

The whistle had no effect on Boru, now veering away from the carriages with George on his heels and Teddy not far behind. The duke's coachman leapt down from his box to assist them, and Silas was helping Lady Clymore from the phaeton. Fear clutched at Betsy's heart as it had in Berkeley Square as she watched the terrified hound lengthen the distance between his pursuers. If they didn't catch him within the next few yards, they never would.

"Don't let him get away!" she shouted, gathering up her shredded skirts to join the chase.

She'd taken no more than half a running step when a firm grip closed on her left elbow and yanked her around. Nearly pulled off her feet by the abrupt change in direction, she gave a squeak of surprise that ended in a gasp of astonishment when she found herself grasped by the elbows in the Duke of Braxton's hands. His eyes looked glazed, as if he were very sleepy or very foxed; the fiery imprint of her knuckles on his chin was already beginning to bruise.

"Not so fast, my lady," he growled. "I've yet to grant you forgiveness for loosening every tooth in my head."

Panic welled in Betsy's breast as his grip tightened and pulled her closer. She was not afraid of the fury glittering in his narrowed, blue-green eyes, but of the sudden rush of warmth his touch sent flooding through her body.

"Please, Your Grace," she pleaded shakily. "I

must see to Boru. He is frightened and unused to the city."

So was Charles. He felt disjointed, as if he were watching himself from a distance—somewhere beyond the damnable ringing in his ears and the dull, sick pounding in his head. God help him, but she was *more* lovely than Aphrodite. Even with leaves in her hair, dirt on her nose—and her hooks into Teddy.

"It occurs to me, my lady, that I could solve the problem you seem intent on becoming by having you taken into charge for trying to kill me."

"Then you would look the veriest fool," Betsy retorted, lifting her chin defiantly, "for I was only trying to cut you loose."

"It's far too late for that," Charles told her, for he knew quite suddenly that it was.

Just as surely as her monstrous pet had tangled and all but strangled him in kite strings, just as easily as she'd captured Teddy, she'd trapped him, too, in her web of gossamer hair and summer-sky-blue eyes. The realization brought with it a wave of light-headedness that rocked Charles on his feet. He mistook it for dizziness caused by his fall, but when his unsteady swaying drew Betsy closer, he recognized it for what it was.

"Let me show you why," he said, pulling her into his arms—and for the first time in his life giving in completely to temptation.

The kiss caught Betsy off-balance as well as off-guard. One moment her feet were firmly planted on the leafy turf, the next they were not. As Hyde Park spun away in a dazzling spiral of sensation, she closed her eyes and clung to the only grounding point she had, the Duke of Braxton's mouth pressed hungrily against hers. She was falling, metaphorically she thought, into the depths and aching sweetness of the kiss, until her shoulder collided roughly with something solid and warm and the smoky fragrance of dying leaves burst in her nostrils.

The impact dragged her mouth free of Charles's and opened her eyes. They *had* fallen—at least the duke had—in a lush windsweep of jewel-toned leaves beneath the oak tree holding his kite captive. His shoulder had cushioned her fall, and she lay, Betsy realized with a shocked gasp, almost completely on top of him, still locked in his embrace.

"I've been a fool," Charles said, his voice deep and wondrous. "A bloody damned fool."

"No, Your Grace. You merely suffered a blow to your head," Betsy replied quaveringly. "A rather nasty one, I fear, when Boru knocked you senseless."

"Would that he had done so years ago!"

Laughing, Charles easily reversed their positions, in the process crushing her poke bonnet beneath her shoulder blades. Betsy scarcely felt it, or the tug of the ribands at her throat, so stunned was she by the awareness of the warmth and length of Charles's body pressed against hers.

Looming over her on one elbow, he raised his free hand and smudged the dirt from her nose. The graze of his fingertips and the tender smile on his face chased shivers of alarm up Betsy's spine.

" 'What life is there, what delight,' " he murmured to her dreamily, " 'without golden Aphrodite?' "

"There won't be *any* for *either* of us," Betsy told

him, her heart banging at the fevered gleam in his eyes as she pushed her flattened palms against his chest, "if you do not, Your Grace, let me up *this second.*"

"Call me Braxton." Catching her right hand in his left, Charles pressed it into the leaves behind her head, gently traced the delicacy of her wrist and the softness of her skin with his thumb. "No, call me Charles."

Betsy wanted to call for help, but there was none, she saw, as she twisted her head desperately away from him. The carriages stood empty at the foot of the slope, Teddy and his reinforcements vanished in pursuit of Boru. There was not so much as a passerby to come to her aid.

Not one that Betsy could see, at any rate, and Julian Dameron had no interest in aiding anyone but himself.

Chapter Twelve

The trick, of course, was how best to turn the tender scene unfolding before him to his advantage. Dashing to Betsy's rescue from the stand of smooth, gray-barked young beeches screening him from view on the edge of the green occurred to Julian, but since he doubted her gratitude would be great enough to agree on the spot to marry him, he rejected the notion.

Their voices had carried sufficiently, despite the wind, to identify Betsy's seducer as the Duke of Braxton. Julian briefly considered using the pistol tucked in his waistband on Charles, though his original intent when he'd borrowed it from the hackney driver, leaving him with orders to wait out of sight around the curve in the road, was to use it on Boru. He'd even thought momentarily of shooting Lady Clymore to remove that obstacle from his path, but she'd nipped away too quickly on the arm of her coachman.

The upstart Earl of Clymore had no real desire to harm any of God's creatures other than Boru, he only wanted Betsy and her blunt. That the thought of murder had even entered his head disturbed him, for it was an indication of his desperation and the hot pursuit of the cent-per-centers. If he did not come about soon, the treacherous and unforgiving River Tick would cast him upon the rocky shores of poverty.

In the Blue Saloon in Berkeley Square he'd felt certain the Duke of Braxton's interest in Betsy was nothing but a hum. But now, as Julian watched Charles catch her chin and turn her face toward his, he was not so certain of the duke's intent. Or of Betsy's response.

But neither was she, pinned and panicked beneath Charles. The trace of his fingertips along the curve of her jaw sent shivers racing everywhere. Steeling herself against them, she jerked her chin free of his hand and glared at him. "I prefer to call you Your Grace," she said coldly, "for I am certain you have no idea what you are doing."

"I have never been more certain of anything," Charles murmured, brushing the tip of his thumb across her lower lip. "But you are right that you should not call me Charles. You should call me Chas."

Loosing his hold on her flung-back wrist, he cupped her face and bent his head to kiss her. With all her strength, Betsy tried to push him off, tried to twist away from him, but he was far too strong. Tears sprang in the corners of her squeezed-shut eyes as his mouth closed over hers, tears of anger, humiliation, and wrenching despair.

The poor addled man hadn't a clue what he was doing. He'd suffered a blow to the head and mistaken her for Aphrodite, just as her father had mistaken her for her long-dead mother after his fatal fall from his hunter. It had given the dying earl comfort in his last hours to cling to her hand and call her Sylvia, but there was no solace in the Duke of Braxton's impassioned confusion. For Betsy, too, had suffered a blow, one most cruel—to her heart.

Flinging her arms wide, she groped for something solid, a clump of grass, a tree root, anything she could use to pull herself free. But there were only leaves, handfuls and handfuls that crumbled to dust at her touch, until her fingers closed on the hard, sharp corner of her last resort. What irony, Betsy thought, as she fumbled to grasp the book in both hands, that Ovid should be my savior.

The solid *thwack* of the expensively bound and therefore heavy volume on the duke's crown, the bleat of pain and surprise he gave as he reeled back on an elbow and clapped a hand to his head, drew a grin and a chortle of relish from Julian. Watching Betsy surge to her feet and round on the duke in a swirl of muddied-pink muslin, cheeks flaming, eyes flashing, her hair snarled with burnished leaves, he made a note to forbid books in the house once they were wed.

"Bloody hell!" Clenching his teeth and clutching his temples, Charles raised his knees and thrust his elbows upon them. "That's twice today you've hit me!"

"Come near me again and I'll make it three!" Betsy warned, a curl loosened from the cluster pinned to the top of her head drooping over her eye as she cocked the book threateningly above her left shoulder.

"You try my patience, lady." Lifting his head from his hands, Charles meant to glare at her, but could only squint painfully in the blinding dazzle of the sunbeams streaming through the oak branches. "Once I can forgive, but twice—"

Fairly growling the last word, he made a fist of

his right hand against the ground and levered himself to his feet. Backing hastily away, Betsy swung the book as hard as she could, but it *whooshed* through nothing but air and spun her around. In midpirouette, her squashed bonnet came sailing over her shoulder and into her eyes. She flung it away and saw Charles fall forward onto his buckled knees.

"Since I am unable at the moment to stand," he said, swaying woozily from side to side, "it appears that wringing your lovely neck will have to wait."

Expelling the breath she hadn't realized she'd drawn and held in a long sigh of relief, Betsy lowered the book. Cautiously tucking the errant curl behind her ear, she watched Charles lift a shaky hand to his head.

"Are you all right, Your Grace?"

"I have asked you to at least call me Braxton, and yes, I am fine. Perfectly."

He raised his right arm to steady himself against the oak tree, which stood, unfortunately, at least a foot away. Betsy's first impulse was to rush to his aid, but instead she bit her lip and winced sympathetically as his palm pushed thin air and he keeled over on his side. When he righted himself and sat back on his hands, legs spread in front of him and breathing hard, she curved the fingers of her right hand against her breast and resisted the urge to sweep back the dark hair tumbling over his forehead.

Neither the nuance of the gesture nor the catch of her lip between her teeth went unnoticed by Julian. Unease made his jaws clamp and his fingers close around the butt of the gun as he inched closer to the edge of the trees and strained to listen.

"You . . . could . . . at . . . least," Charles panted, "help . . . me . . . rise."

"I think it wiser not to, Your Grace." Betsy backed further away and knelt to pick up her emptied reticule.

Something crunched beneath her right slipper as she did so. Tugging her skirts aside and lifting her heel, she plucked her grandfather's spectacles out of the leaves. The left lens was shattered, the earpiece hopelessly twisted.

"Drat!" Betsy stuffed them unhappily into her bag. "Now I shall have to get another pair."

"How charming that you wear spectacles!" Charles exclaimed, a delighted grin on his face. "I do as well!"

"I don't wear them, Your Grace. I merely carry them in my reticule."

Sifting through the windfall, Betsy uncovered her grandfather's snuffbox. A bright scarlet oak leaf trembled by one point from the lid. She pinched it free between her thumb and forefinger, then let it go, her gaze locking with Charles's as she watched it flutter away. His lips were parted and his eyes wide with astonishment.

"You take snuff as well?"

"Hardly. I carry it in my reticule merely for the effect, as I do—or *did*—my grandfather's spectacles."

Charles blinked at her bewilderedly. "Eh?"

"Never mind, Your Grace." Betsy sighed and dropped the snuffbox into her bag. "It is a long story, and would only make your head worse for hearing it."

"There is nothing wrong with my head," he

snapped irritably, "and you may tell the tale when I call upon you on the morrow."

Betsy smiled and arched a dubious eyebrow. "I don't think so, Your Grace."

"You don't think what?"

"I do not think you will call upon me, on the morrow or any other day."

"Now see here—" Charles began, grunting with effort as he pushed with both arms and tried again to stand.

Betsy scrambled to her feet but needlessly, for the duke could not even budge himself from the ground. Gasping for breath, he fell back on the heels of his hands, an angry frown and a gleam of perspiration on his face.

"That tears it!" Charles smashed a furious fist into the ground. "With your temperament, lady, I fear I must forbid you books once we are wed."

In the trees, Julian bit his knuckle and nearly swooned. It wasn't a hum. It was the truth, the awful truth. Grasping a beech sapling for support, he swung away from the clearing. The rocks loomed closer, larger, and sharper than ever. Hell and damnation. He'd inherited an earldom, but not a single bloody farthing to support it.

Julian raked an unsteady hand through his hair and cursed himself again for allowing Lady Clymore to bring Betsy to London. Wretched old clutchfist. She'd made it clear she would not allow the estates to fall into disrepair, but not one penny more would she part with. He could mortgage them, he supposed, but he'd have to shoot the countess first, for she would surely shoot him when she found it out.

Again, Julian's fingers strayed to the pistol. Or shoot Braxton before he offered for Betsy, for as things stood now, he'd be risking the only thing of value he possessed—his unblemished reputation as a gentleman—if he refused the duke. If only he'd come to town sooner. If only he hadn't underestimated Betsy's charms, though in truth he still hadn't the foggiest notion what they were. If only . . . if only—*if only Betsy would refuse him*. The wondrous but remote possibility drew Julian up short and spun him around.

"Nothing to say?" Charles prodded smugly. "Excellent. Then we shall deal very well together."

"No, Your Grace, we will *not*," Betsy replied staunchly. "And if I thought for an instant you had any inkling of what you are saying, I would, indeed, have a great deal to say."

"Damn and blast it! I cannot stand, but I am not an idiot! I am not the least bit—" Charles broke off, fist raised to pound the ground again. "You've heard me called His Dottiness. That's what this is. That's why you think I'm a raving lunatic."

"Yes, Your Grace. I mean, no, that's not why."

"What then?" Charles ground out exasperatedly.

"Please, Your Grace. I've no wish to further humiliate either of us." Betsy gathered up her bedraggled skirts. "Let me find Teddy and your coachman. You should lie down and rest, perhaps take a draft of laudanum. It will help you to sleep and to forget your intention to call upon me."

"Don't you dare move!"

The thunder in his voice—and the groan of agony that followed—turned Betsy in her tracks as she wheeled away to find and fetch Teddy. Charles was gritting his teeth and clutching his head again. What little Betsy could see of his face between his fingers was a frightening chalky-gray. Her tender heart overcame her sense and she ran to him, falling on her knees at his side.

"You should not shout," she said, pushing her hands on his shoulders and trying to make him lie down. "It will only make the blood pound in your head."

"No, lady. *You* make my blood pound." Charles let go of his head and caught her arms, his gaze and his grip overwarm.

With fever rather than ardor, Betsy was certain. His eyes were glassy with it, his throat flushed.

" 'Not fire nor stars,' " he said to her, " 'have stronger bolts than those of Aphrodite.' "

"I am *not* Aphrodite! Any more than you are Euripides!"

"Well, of course I'm not!" Charles struggled indignantly up on his hands. "I was merely trying to be romantic."

"I think it more likely, Your Grace, that your brain is so scrambled you don't even know who I am!"

"My brain is *not* scrambled!" He shouted, winced, and sucked a breath through clenched teeth. "Pray tell me why you keep insisting otherwise. *Softly*, I beg you, lest I disgrace myself on your slippers."

"It was so with my father," Betsy said, sotto voce, as she knelt beside him. "He, too, suffered a blow on the head and breathed his last believing I was my mother."

"God in heaven." Charles swept a hand over his eyes, then fixed the soberest gaze he could muster on Betsy. It was difficult, for her features kept blurring. "I've had a nasty crack on the noggin, I'll grant you, but even so, I can assure you—most *fervently*, my lady—that it would be impossible to mistake you for anyone else."

"Prove it, then. Who am I?"

"Clearly," Charles replied, leaning wearily back on his hands, "you are my downfall."

It was just as well she'd laid Ovid's *Amores* aside when she'd picked up her reticule, Betsy thought furiously, else she might have bashed him with it again. She still had her tiny little fists, but the knuckles of her right hand ached abominably. And so did her heart.

"Spanish coin, I'm sure." Scraping together what little remained of her dignity, Betsy rose. "I think it safe to say you are well on your way back to being yourself, Your Grace. Good day."

Dropping him a curtsey, she lifted her nose and her skirts and fled in search of Teddy.

"Damn and blast it, come back here!" he bellowed.

But Betsy only ran faster, leaves spilling from the battered bonnet against her shoulder blades. Gritting his teeth against the sickening, thudding ring in his ears, Charles banged his fists against the ground in frustration.

"Temper, temper, my lord." Julian *tsk*ed, grinning with glee, and waited to see if Braxton would be so undignified as to cast up his accounts in the middle of Hyde Park.

When he rolled over on his back and flung an arm over his eyes, Julian sighed with disappointment and made his way back through the trees to the hired hackney. The driver, a scruffy-looking fellow with several days beard blackening his features, turned in his box as Julian handed up his pistol.

"Missed 'im, eh?"

"Mind your horses," the earl replied curtly as he opened the coach door and climbed inside. "Keep straight to this road and take me to White's."

"Aye, guv," the driver responded, clucking his horses forward without complaint.

The longer, more circuitous route would ensure that Julian's presence went unknown by Betsy, for it would not do at all for her to know he'd witnessed her seduction by the Duke of Braxton. Not yet, at least, Julian thought, pursing his lips as he leaned against the threadbare squabs and considered how best—if at all—to make use of what he had seen and heard.

So long as she believed the duke's screws had been sufficiently loosened by the clout he'd taken on the head, he would keep the incident to himself. But if Braxton were able to convince her otherwise, or if it proved the duke was not after all dicked in the nob, then, Julian decided, he would be forced to reveal what he knew. First to Lady Clymore, then to Betsy if the countess proved arbitrary, and if necessary, to the whole of the ton.

Blackmail was an ugly word, but so was *poverty*. If he could not otherwise win Betsy's promise, then he would extort it. Not without compunction, but the means justified the end. He would find a way to make it up to her, though precisely how he hadn't a clue— until the hackney rolled out of the park onto Knightsbridge and he saw Boru, tongue lolling and kite strings snarled in his tail, galloping along the verge.

Neither his mistress, Lady Clymore, or the duke's pup of a brother were anywhere to be seen. A perfectly brilliant plan for redeeming himself in Betsy's eyes sprang into Julian's head.

Snatching up his walking stick, he thumped the roof of the coach, then leaned out the window and shouted to the driver, "Follow that dog!"

Chapter Thirteen

*P*erhaps logic and reason *didn't* solve everything, Charles thought, as he lay battered and aching beneath the oak tree. Emotion didn't, either; he was certain of that—for it was the very thing that had landed him flat on his back, marveling at the fact that he'd kissed Lady Elizabeth Keaton. Not once, God help him, but twice.

Could it be that this was his mother's meaning when she'd said he wasn't half so clever as he thought? Or was his brain really scrambled?

Whether it was or not, he would do the gentlemanly thing. Just as soon as he could stand without wanting to retch he would call upon Lady Clymore and ask permission to pay his addresses. She would accept, of course, and so would Betsy, if for no other reason than to escape her mushroom cousin.

It hit him then, as suddenly and as painfully as another clout on the head, that perhaps *he* had been Lady Elizabeth's quarry all along, that Teddy was but a lure.

The thought made Charles want to retch again, and he rolled over on his stomach with a groan. No, it wasn't possible. She'd bashed him once— no, twice—and threatened to a third time. If she planned to trap him into marriage, she wouldn't have beaten him off. Or had she done so *knowing* she could count on him to do the proper thing?

There was only one way to find out—present himself posthaste in Berkeley Square. But first, he had to get up. Gritting his teeth, Charles struggled up on his elbows, his head clanging and clashing and— No, it wasn't his head. He lifted his chin, breathing hard and blinking, and spied the cause of the clatter—the remnants of his wind device dangling and banging against the bole of the oak tree from what was left of one of his kites.

"Damn and blast," he swore breathlessly.

"Sorry, Chas," Teddy said, dropping on his haunches and into his line of vision. "It appears to be beyond repair."

Charles squinted at his brother. The lad's coat was snagged with leaves, the buttons gone, his cravat and waistcoat torn, and his lawn shirt more green than white.

"So do you, halfling. What the devil happened?"

Easing himself to the ground, Teddy crossed his booted ankles and looped his arms loosely and tiredly around his knees. "Took a header—no, several, actually—trying to catch Boru."

Charles blinked to clear the spots swimming at the corners of his eyes. "Trying?"

"Got clean away on us. Wouldn't have if Lady Clymore's gouty foot hadn't given out on her." Teddy rubbed a tear in the left leg of his pantaloons where a patch of barked skin showed above the top of his dirt-caked Hessian. "Or if Lady Betsy had come along in time."

Guilt and nausea washed over Charles as he struggled higher up on his left elbow. "Where is

127

she? I believe I owe her an apology for detaining her."

At the very damned least, he thought, despising himself. The hound was a menace, but she was devoted to the bloody creature. And she had begged him to let her go.

"I loaned her my curricle and she's gone with her footman to search for Boru." Teddy left off rubbing his shin, leaned his elbow on his knee, and blinked wearily at Charles. "Hope to blazes they find him before some Cit mistakes him for a wolf and shoots him."

"That's it, spoon it on thick." Charles gritted his teeth and pushed himself up on his hand.

Teddy raised his head puzzledly. "Spoon what on?"

"Never mind." Charles peered at the carriages drawn up on the verge of the greensward. He couldn't quite make out if there were two or four. "Lady Clymore?"

"Her coachman and Fletcher are bringing her," Teddy said, turning his head to follow his brother's gaze, just as the servants came around the curve in the road bearing the countess between them on their clasped and crossed hands.

Vauxhall or Drury Lane would be hard-pressed to provide a better entertainment, Charles thought, watching the burly coachmen huff and puff while Lady Clymore clung to them with her elbows crooked round their necks. Thank God it was no where near five o'clock, when the park would be awash with the crème de la crème.

And what of Betsy? Charles's pulse quickened with dread at the thought. What if she didn't find Boru by then? What if she returned to the scene of his disappearance at the zenith of the fashionable hour in her torn and muddied pelisse, her crushed poke bonnet flapping along behind her?

"Quickly, halfling. What's the hour?"

Teddy fished his watch from his waistcoat and sprang it open. Pieces of the shattered face tinkled out onto his palm, along with the broken hour hand. "At whatever moment I fell upon your birthday gift, it was half-past something."

"Bloody marvelous." Charles pushed himself off the ground, wobbling as a wave of vertigo rolled over him.

"Should you be standing?" Teddy sprang to his feet and tucked a shoulder beneath his. "You look a bit rum."

"Kind of you to notice." Charles arched a wry brow. "Kinder still for you to say so."

"Your eyes look—odd." Teddy peered at him intently. "Are you quite yourself, Chas?"

"No, thank God." Charles drew and exhaled a deep breath. Standing wasn't so bad, now that he'd managed it. "I'm a new man."

"How is that possible?"

"I'm not entirely sure," Charles replied, slowly, as he considered the matter. "But I'm not the man Boru knocked unconscious."

Teddy's eyebrows drew together worriedly. "Who are you, then?"

Bonnie Prince Charlie, Charles wanted to reply, for he felt suddenly euphoric. His head still pounded unmercifully, but the vertigo had given way to a giddy sense of well-being. Yet Teddy looked so grave he dared not be flippant.

"Don't worry, halfling," he assured him. "I've not

taken leave of my senses. I've merely rediscovered them."

"I was not aware you'd lost them."

"Neither was I, but it seems perfectly clear to me now that I must have somewhere along the way."

Teddy's brows leapt in alarm. "I think you should sit down again, Chas."

"Once I've had a word with Lady Clymore." He nodded at the countess, now seated in the yellow phaeton and gesturing urgently in his direction. "While I'm at it, I want you to gather up Lady Betsy's reticule, the dagger, snuffbox, and anything else of hers you can find among the leaves." He lifted his arm from Teddy's shoulders and planted a finger in his neckcloth. "Discreetly, halfling. I want a thorough look at her rackety collection before I return it."

Young Lord Theodore's eyes lit with interest. "As Your Grace wishes."

As he wheeled back to the oak tree, Charles drew a steadying breath and struck off across the greensward. Walking was more of a challenge than standing, but he managed the distance, slowly and carefully, the ringing in his ears subsiding as he drew near enough to the phaeton for the countess's features to coalesce into one face.

"My apologies, Lady Clymore." Firmly but surreptitiously, Charles grasped the front wheel and made her a small bow. "Had I any idea Teddy would loan Lady Elizabeth his curricle, I would have forbade it."

"Oh, bother that," the dowager said, with a sniff. "Prinny himself could not have gainsaid Betsy. She'll be safe enough with George until Silas and I join the hunt."

"May I offer my services, ma'am? If we split three ways surely the hound can be run to ground in short order."

Lady Clymore notched a brow at him. "No offense, Braxton, but you seem hardly able to stand."

"I'm in no worse shape than you, my lady. I can sit as well in my carriage as you can in yours."

Lady Clymore inclined her chin. "It is kind of you, then."

Hardly that, Charles thought, with another twinge of guilt. It was the least he could do.

"I trust you will be well enough to stand up with me tomorrow evening at the Countess Featherston's ball."

If Lady Clymore felt any surprise at being asked to leave the ranks of the dowagers her face did not show it. Rather, she eyed Charles sharply. "Without a doubt I shall be. But what of you?"

"I shall be right as rain and pleased to lead you out," Charles drawled, with a shrug he hoped the countess would take for indifference. "And Lady Elizabeth, of course, if she has room on her card."

"Of course." Lady Clymore's gaze narrowed. "And Teddy? Will he be attending?"

"I should think."

"Then it is time you and I had a coze, Braxton."

"At your convenience, my lady." Grasping the wheel again for balance, Charles made her another bow. "On the morrow?"

"If it is at all convenient, I would prefer this evening. Shall we say eight of the clock?"

It was a summons, despite the courteous phrasing, and clearly to do with Teddy. Not surprising, since the little scamp was always up to something.

"As my lady wishes," Charles said, nodding his

acceptance. "May I suggest that you and your coachman concentrate your efforts on locating Lady Betsy. Fletcher—" Charles paused to signal his coachman—"and Teddy and I will scour every inch of the park. I further suggest we meet here in an hour's time to widen the search if necessary."

"Sensible. Let us make it so."

The coachmen conferred for a moment, then Silas climbed up on his seat and clucked to his team. Once the phaeton had bowled away in a vivid sweep of leaves, Teddy came pelting up with Betsy's reticule clanking over his arm.

"Damned thing's heavy," he complained. "Weighs near half a stone, I'll wager."

Charles took it from him, incredulity widening his eyes. "What the deuce has she got in here?"

"Best look for yourself. Are we off to find Boru?"

"We are," Charles said, turning toward Fletcher and directing him to make a slow circuit of the park.

Once he and Teddy had taken seats facing each other and the carriage was underway, Charles up-ended the reticule on the deep blue velvet squabs. "Bloody hell," he muttered, lifting Edward Keaton's pistol gingerly in two fingers.

"It's been disabled," Teddy told him, shifting his attention to the window.

"Since she can't shoot anyone with it, then she must carry the pistol, too, for effect." Charles laid it aside and picked up a leather-bound book. Without his spectacles, and with his vision still somewhat blurred, he had to lift it nearly to his nose to read the title stamped in Latin and gilt letters.

"Bloody *damned* hell!" he exclaimed, as the words swam into focus, and hastily stuffed the book

132

beneath the coat he'd shed earlier and left on the squabs.

"Found friend Ovid, eh?" Teddy gave him a roguish grin. "Lady Betsy refers to him as her last resort."

Against would-be seducers, no doubt, Charles thought, his head pounding viciously at the memory of the thick tome colliding with his skull. "It could be worse," he said ruefully. "She could be able to read it."

Teddy leaned forward and bent his elbows on his knees. "Oh, but she *can*."

The duke's right hand froze halfway to his thudding temple. *"What?"*

"Bit of a bluestocking is our Lady Betsy," Teddy informed him, with a wicked wag of his brows.

"Hides it well, doesn't she?" Charles swiped his hand over his mouth to hide the grin quivering there at the irony of being smashed over the head with Ovid.

For Teddy's sake he strove to appear as outraged, as indignant, as he would have just a day—nay, just an hour ago—but simply could not manage it. "What a morning for revelations," he said, and burst into laughter.

Teddy cocked his head curiously. "You aren't furious?"

"Heavens, no." Charles knuckled mirthful tears from his eyes. "I'm sure Lady Clymore would be if she knew, but I've no intention of telling her."

To keep from falling off it, Teddy sat back on the banquette. "You *don't*?"

"I *do* intend to tell Betsy." He plucked Ovid out from under his coat and arched a brow. "This isn't *at all* the thing for a duchess to lug about in her reticule."

For a moment, Teddy simply stared at him, his mouth falling slowly open. Then he gave a cock-a-whoop shout and leapt across the carriage. He intended to clap Charles on the back, but his sudden lurch rocked the springs and pitched him instead onto his brother's lap.

"Steady, halfling," Charles said, with a laugh, catching him in his arms.

"You dull old stick!" Teddy crowed, clinging to his neck. "You've made me the happiest of fellows!"

"I believe *I'm* supposed to say that." Charles grinned and dumped his brother onto the banquette beside him. "But not until I've asked and Lady Elizabeth accepts."

"You've not gone down on your knee?"

"I intend to speak to Lady Clymore—and Betsy—this evening."

"Oh, I see." Heaving a deflated sigh, Teddy scooted across the squabs to the window. "In that case, I wouldn't pin my hopes on it, if I were you."

"Why not?" Charles asked suspiciously.

"Because Betsy has taken you in complete disgust," Teddy said, sliding a cool glance over his shoulder. "And since you lured her into Lady Pinchon's garden last evening I shouldn't wonder."

"I did not *lure* her anywhere," Charles denied vehemently. "I said *pardon*, which she mistook for *garden*."

"There's nothing wrong with Betsy's hearing. It's Lady Pinchon who's deaf." Teddy *tsk*ed. "Really, Chas. How low."

"She had lamb's wool stuffed in her ears,"

Charles retorted. "Couldn't hear a damn thing I said!"

"Then how did she end up with your coat?"

"I loaned it to her when I tore her gown."

"Charles!" Teddy gasped, falling back into the corner of the banquette with a hand pressed to his cravat.

"I stepped on her *hem*," Charles snapped, a muscle leaping in his jaw. "In the *foyer*, mind you, *not* the garden."

"Nonetheless," Teddy said stiffly, as he swung back to the window, "I'm sure that's the reason Betsy said she'd clout you with her reticule if you came near her again."

"She *did* that," Charles muttered ruefully, "but not with her reticule."

"She stuck to it, too, even when I pointed out the advantages to leading Julian Dameron to believe she was on the verge of receiving an offer from you."

"What do you mean, you *led* him?"

"I had to do *something*," Teddy responded over his shoulder, "for he was there when I called this morning in Berkeley Square, ensconced in the Blue Saloon as smug as a cat in cream."

"Why drag me into it?" Charles demanded angrily. "Why not tell him you and Betsy plan to elope?"

"Because," he replied, slowly and patiently, as if addressing the village slowtop, "that was nothing but a hum."

"No more a hum than the absolute clanker that *I* am about to offer for the silly chit!"

"But you *are*, Chas. You just said so. Not that

she'll have you," Teddy added, with a shrug. "Especially if you keep calling her a silly chit."

"Fletcher!" Charles roared, grasping the strap and swinging out the window to keep himself from committing fratricide. "Stop here!" he commanded, kicking the door open before the carriage had come to a complete stop. "We'd best go afoot, else we'll never find the wretched beast."

"Yes, Chas," Teddy murmured dutifully, smothering a slyly satisfied smile as he scrambled out of the carriage behind him.

As he jumped to the ground, Charles grabbed a fistful of his collar. "Come along, little sapskull," he growled, striding purposefully toward the Grosvenor Gate.

"Why've you flown into the boughs now?" Teddy demanded, stumbling along beside him as best he could.

"You *dare* ask why?" Charles fumed as he stalked across the greensward with Teddy in tow. "You admit your plan to elope was nothing but a banger, then you *claim* you had no choice but to mislead Dameron into thinking I intend to offer for Betsy Keaton!" He came to an abrupt halt and yanked his brother around to face him. "Are you sure *you* put the idea of misleading him into Betsy's head, or was it already there?"

"Oh, I *say*—"

"Answer me." Charles twisted his hand around Teddy's neckcloth and pulled him up on his toes. "The truth, or I'll have your guts for garters."

"Well, I—" He broke off as he caught a glimpse over Charles's shoulder of the urchin boy and his little brown dog peeking out of a nearby bank of shrubbery.

"Ted-dy," Charles growled, twisting another length of his cravat around his hand.

"In the bushes," he croaked, hardly able to breathe.

"Boru?" Charles let go and spun sharply on his heel.

"No." Teddy breathed deeply and rubbed his throat. "The urchin boy who helped us find him."

"Maybe he's seen the silly beast." Charles started eagerly forward, but Teddy clamped a hand on his elbow.

"Slowly and quietly," he whispered. "He's skittish and quick off the mark."

Nodding, Charles tucked one hand in his waistcoat pocket, and side by side, they sauntered casually toward the clump of bushes. When the boy bolted, Teddy snatched the string tied to his dog's collar, and Charles caught his ear. Not hard enough to hurt him, just hard enough to hold him.

"Half a crown for a moment of your time, young fellow."

"Bugger off," the boy spat, twisting his head around as best he could to glare at Charles.

"We won't hurt you," Teddy said, stepping forward so the boy could see him. "Remember me? Lady Betsy and I saved you from the man who beat you with his cane. Her dog has gone missing again. Have you seen him?"

The boy craned his neck again to peer up at Charles. "I seen a jarvey take 'im up."

Letting go of his ear, Charles took his coin purse from his waistcoat pocket, fished out a half crown, and dropped it in the boy's filthy palm. "Very well, then. You may go."

The boy snatched the dog's string from Teddy,

turned to run, but hesitated. "Ye'll tell 'er Ladyship?"

"You have my word," the duke assured him solemnly.

" 'Right then, guv."

Charles watched the boy wrap the string around
his wrist and dash away with the little dog limping
beside him, then turned toward Teddy with a curiously cocked eyebrow. "What the devil is a jarvey?"

"A hackney driver," Teddy replied, looking as
puzzled as Charles.

Chapter Fourteen

"'A hackney driver'?" Charles repeated incredulously. "Are you quite sure?"

"'Course I am," Teddy replied archly. "I've not been rusticating this age. The question is what the devil does a jarvey want with Boru?"

"Ransom, I'll wager," Charles replied darkly, as they started back the way they'd come. "Boru is a hound of obvious breeding. No manners," he added dryly, "but breeding."

As they neared the carriage, a blue high-perch phaeton bowled past at a high rate of speed, showering them in dust and upchurned leaves. Fletcher shouted and shook his whip; Teddy glared at the reckless young blood at the ribbons.

"You could say the same for many of the ton, as well."

"I wish we knew the hour." Charles waved away another swirl of grit as a dark green curricle drawn by a familiar pair of blacks rocketed past in the wake of the phaeton.

"Betsy!" he and Teddy shouted in unison.

Her ruined bonnet tumbled over her shoulder as she saw them and hauled on the leathers. On the seat beside her, as she turned the spirited, still-ready-to-run team in a smart circle, George loosened the death grip he'd fastened on the side of the curricle.

"Have you seen Boru?" Betsy called worriedly.

She looked nearly as winded as the blacks to Charles, her hair as snarled as the manes they tossed as they pranced and chafed under the tight rein. Her face was pale but for ruddied spots of color in her cheeks, her luminous eyes huge and anxious.

"No," he replied, catching the right leader's bridle, "but we did run to ground a young urchin of your acquaintance who says he saw Boru taken up in a hackney."

"Oh, no," she breathed, wilting visibly on the seat of the curricle.

"I shall post a handbill," Charles told her gently. "The scoundrel will come round soon enough with Boru and his hand out for a fat reward."

"The *devil* you will!" Betsy sprang straight on the seat, her face awash with fresh, angry color. "I'll find him *myself!* If I have to waylay every hackney in London!"

Taking the ribbons in one hand, she reached for the whip with the other. Before she could lift it, Charles clamped his fingers on her wrist.

"I think not, my lady. Not in your present state."

"Unhand me." Betsy's eyes flashed. "There is nothing wrong with *my state.* Past, future, or *present.*"

"Oh, no?" Charles signed to George.

The footman nodded and jumped down to help Teddy hold the blacks. Then Charles shook the ribbons free of Betsy's ungloved right hand. She sucked a breath between clenched teeth as the air hit the raw flesh in the curve of her thumb and forefinger.

"With this hand, my lady," Charles said, turning her wrist to blow softly at the blister welling there, "you'll find it devilish difficult to use your fan at the Countess Featherston's ball tomorrow evening."

Despite the feathery chill fluttering up her arm, his mention of the affair reminded Betsy that Teddy had made a to-do of it earlier—and that the Earl of Clymore had left Berkeley Square in a tearing hurry and a hackney.

"Julian!" she gasped, causing Charles to lift his head quizzically. "My cousin, the Earl of Clymore, called upon us this morning in a hackney."

"That's so," Teddy chimed in.

"Did the boy mention Julian?" Betsy asked him.

"No, just the jarvey. Had he seen his lordship I'm sure he would've remarked upon it, since when we came upon them on the flagway Dameron was thrashing the boy with his cane."

Loosing Betsy's wrist, Charles prudently lifted the ribbons from her grasp and wrapped them around the brake. "Then it appears we are in search of two beasts."

At the muscle leaping in his jaw and the vicious twist he gave the leathers, Betsy chose to forgive his veiled insult to Boru. She rubbed her wrist, which still throbbed from his touch, against her skirt.

"Boru detests Julian, but he would happily go anywhere with anyone else. Especially as frightened as he was."

"Do you know Clymore's direction?" Charles asked, squelching a fresh qualm of guilt.

"Sadly, no. He is, I believe, just arrived in London."

"A mushroom can't be that hard to find," Teddy put in. "And if all else fails, he may return to Berkeley Square to take up residence as he threatened."

"Hopefully so." Betsy brightened, but not much, as the yellow phaeton, with her grandmother and Silas aboard, approached from the opposite direction and came to a halt.

Once the situation was explained to Lady Clymore—mostly by Charles, but with additions by Teddy and Betsy as he helped her down from his curricle and into the phaeton—it was agreed that a handbill would be printed and posted, and the search for Boru suspended until such time as Julian Dameron could be located. Or he presented himself again in Berkeley Square.

"And he will, most assuredly," Lady Clymore opined emphatically.

And ominously, thought Betsy, quelling the fear she felt at the idea of Boru in Julian's hands. Not literally, of course, for he would have to depend on a hireling such as a hackney driver to handle Boru. But to what purpose?

"Until this evening, Lady Clymore." Charles bowed to the countess, but raised his gaze to Betsy. His eyes no longer gleamed with fever and apoplexy, they smoldered with it. "You see, Lady Elizabeth, I do not forget my promises."

"Just this once, Your Grace," she replied coolly, "I think you would be well advised to do so."

"But I cannot." The pang Betsy felt at the smile he gave her as he backed away from the phaeton made her turn her head away until Silas clucked to his grays.

"What was that about?" Lady Clymore asked,

just as Betsy shifted on the squabs to inquire of her grandmother, "Why is His Grace calling upon you this evening?"

"You first," the countess directed sternly. "What promise did Braxton make you and when?"

"Merely a promise to call, Granmama, to hear the tale of how Boru escaped and came to knock him senseless."

"God's teeth!" Lady Clymore clapped a hand to her forehead. "Not again!"

"He was most accommodating," Betsy lied, with only a tiny twinge. "I thought it odd, to say the least, but I'm sure his brain was completely scrambled by the fall."

Lady Clymore lowered her hand and blinked. "How could you tell?"

"He called me by another name, as Papa did. I should not take seriously anything he might say to you, Granmama. The poor man has lost his wits completely." Betsy paused, then asked mildly, "What reason did he give for wishing to call upon you?"

"Impertinent gel," Lady Clymore replied tartly. " 'Twas I who asked Braxton, and the reason is no concern of yours."

"How unfair!" Betsy howled.

"Of course it is unfair, but it is what you deserve for running afoul of Braxton, when you promised—" Her ladyship broke off and again clapped a hand to her brow. "Hell and damnation! The note you sent with his coat! What did you write, you wretched gel?"

"I'd forgotten!" Betsy smiled—no, grinned—with relish at the recollection.

"I'll have the truth, miss," Lady Clymore threatened, "or you will have the birch rod."

"Of course, Granmama," Betsy replied prettily. "I told His Grace he had the manners of a goat."

"You what?" the countess squawked. "You rackety, maggot-headed gel! You shatterbrain! You cotton-headed chit!"

With any luck, Betsy thought, as she listened to her grandmother rain names upon her, the Duke of Braxton would have a similar reaction, and one major worry would be scraped off her dish. Not that she thought for an instant Charles seriously intended to offer for her—not after he'd had a good night's sleep. But knowing that her note would eliminate the possibility of a rash offer he'd regret on the morrow left her mind clear to dwell on Boru and how to get him back. From a hackney driver or Julian, whichever the case might be.

She hoped Charles was right, that a passing jarvey had spied Boru and a fat reward, for she could not fathom why her cousin would want the hound. Other than to dispose of him permanently, and Betsy steadfastly refused to believe even Julian could be so cruel. Returning Boru to turn her up sweet was the most likely possibility, and it was the one Betsy clung to for comfort throughout the long afternoon of writing the handbill and dispatching it for printing, bathing and washing her hair, and helping Lady Clymore's abigail treat her swollen foot.

Hope sustained her until the fall of evening, when the Duke of Braxton's impending visit stirred a flock of butterflies in her stomach. It was also Boru's usual hour for exercise, and it was just possible, Betsy reasoned, that her darling might manage to get himself free of Julian or the hackney driver and make his way home in time for his romp with George. In which case, someone ought to be there to let him in through the gate in the back garden wall.

And if she couldn't be found when Charles called—and he left without seeing her—that would be fine, too.

Throwing a woolen shawl over her shoulders, Betsy crept down the back stairs to the kitchen. Cook was in the scullery, which gave her a clear path to the door. She took it and let herself noiselessly out of the house into the cool and musky-smelling dusk. It was almost, but not quite chill, not yet.

With a minimum of crunching underfoot, Betsy picked her way through the dry leaves scattering the lawn to a fair-sized oak growing near the wall. When she grasped the lowest limb to pull herself up, the bark bit painfully into her blistered hand. Catching her lip in her teeth, she held on, pulled herself up to the first crotch, and from there onto the capped top of the wall. Not as nimbly as she might have the day before, for the muscles in her calves ached and her knees cracked as she sat down.

The wall felt cold beneath her skirts, but no colder than the cobbles would feel beneath Boru's paws if he were still on the loose. Thinking of him wandering the streets, lost and frightened and hungry, brought tears to her eyes. What if he'd gotten away but couldn't find Berkeley Square? What if he never did?

Feeling thoroughly miserable, Betsy gazed at the injured hand cradled in her lap. The blister wept and she could just see the bruises on her knuckles in the fading light. What a wretched day. Of all the people in all of London, why did Charles have to be the man flying a kite on that particular stretch of green?

How hopeful and happy she'd been upon her arrival in London. How simple she'd thought it would be to find a husband and escape Julian. How perfect her plan to be outrageous had seemed. How *naive*, how *idiotic*.

How had it all gone so horribly wrong?

Perhaps it was just bad luck, or the work of the Fates the Greeks prosed on and on about. She'd lost Boru and she'd lost her silly heart to a man who thought her nothing more than a scheming huntress. What a cruel twist that was. He should have called her Diana, not Aphrodite.

Leave it to Charles to know Mimnermus, one of the more obscure poets. Still, she would treasure for the rest of her days the wondrous expression on his face when he'd murmured to her dreamily of life and delight.

"Oh, Charles," Betsy murmured, lifting her fingers and smiling, albeit sadly, at the feel of his name on her lips.

"Me name's Davey," came a small voice from the near darkness below.

Twisting at the waist and leaning on the heels of her hands, Betsy peered into the gloom at the foot of the wall and saw the boy looking up at her with Scraps in his arms. Her heart leapt at the sight of him and the little terrier whining and wagging his tail.

"How do you do, Davey? My name's Betsy."

"That jarvey brung Boru back?"

"No, not yet. I want to thank you for telling my friends what you saw. It was very brave of you."

"T'warn't nothin'," Davey said, with a shrug that ended in a shiver.

"Would you like to come up and sit with me?" Betsy asked, quelling an impulse to jump down and fling her shawl around him. When he drew back a nervous step, she added hastily, "I'm keeping watch for Boru, and would be most pleased to have your company."

He hesitated, shifting from one foot to another. Betsy held herself ready to leap after him if he turned to run. She'd lost Boru, but she would not, by heaven, lose Davey.

"All right, then," he said finally, pronouncing it *roight*.

Swinging herself to the ground via the oak tree, Betsy raced for the gate, half afraid he'd be gone when she opened it. But he wasn't, and she breathed a sigh of relief.

"Your parents won't mind if you're out after dark?"

"Me an' Scraps is orphans," Davey mumbled, ducking his head to scratch the little dog's ears.

"What a small world. So am I."

Davey raised a suspicious glance. "Who's th' ol' crone I seen you with?"

Betsy smothered a grin. "My grandmother."

" 'Er drink gin?"

"No. Does yours?"

Davey ducked his head again. "Did 'fore 'er fell off 'er perch."

"So there's no one to care if you're out alone?"

He raised just his chin and looked at her, his eyes glimmering in the near dark. "No'um."

"There is now." Betsy smiled and offered Davey her hand.

Chapter Fifteen

When Charles arrived in Berkeley Square on the second chime of eight o'clock, Lady Clymore was in the Blue Saloon, a cane leaning against the back of the striped satin settee she sat upon. A tea service rested on the table in front of her, her gouty foot on a small stool beneath it.

"Shall we get straight to it," she asked, waving Charles into a chair placed next to the settee as the butler closed the doors, "or would you like a cup of tea?"

"I prefer to get down to cases," he replied, crossing one knee and resisting the urge he felt to jiggle his foot.

He'd spent the afternoon waving away the laudanum and burned feathers his mother had tried to foist on him in favor of pacing the library and planning what he would say to Lady Clymore. Giving in to the wretched pounding in his head and the occasional wash of vertigo would have been easy, but Charles was determined not to, for it had occurred to him at some point in the long afternoon that the easy path was not always the best path.

"A delightful boy, Teddy," Lady Clymore began, "but somewhat excessive."

"One of the Earnshaw family's less noble traits,

I fear," Charles replied truthfully. "I myself have spent a lifetime fighting the tendency."

"Forgive my plainspeaking, Braxton," Lady Clymore said forthrightly, "but in your case a bit of it might have been just the thing."

"How perceptive." Charles grinned. "Do you know, my lady, that very thing occurred to me this afternoon."

Lady Clymore notched a brow. "It did?"

"Yes, as a matter of fact." Charles's grin twisted wryly. "I regret it took Boru knocking me senseless to make the point, but there you are. Any word of him, by the way?"

"I fear not." The dowager sighed and reached for the teapot. "Much as I loathe the beast, I would give half of all I possess to have him back and see Betsy smile."

So would I, Charles thought, but said sternly, "Don't even think to intimate such a thing when the scoundrel comes seeking his reward."

A knock at the saloon doors lifted Lady Clymore's attention from the tea service. "Yes, Iddings?"

The butler came into the room and shut the doors. "The Earl of Clymore is just arrived, my lady."

"Speaking of scoundrels!" The countess glowered. "Is he come with or without a portmanteau?"

"Without, my lady."

"Pity." Lady Clymore sighed disappointedly.

"Does he have Boru with him?" Charles asked.

If Iddings felt any surprise at the question he did not show it. "No, Your Grace."

"May I suggest you allow me to handle Clymore?" Charles said to the countess. "I may be able to determine if he is responsible for Boru's disappearance."

"Gladly," Lady Clymore agreed, nodding to Iddings as she put down the pot and lifted her filled cup, "for I must own that he vexes me beyond reason."

"My mother tells me you are the devil's own at whist, my lady." Charles leaned toward her on one elbow. "You play with a face the Sphinx itself would envy."

"Does she?" the countess preened. "How kind."

"I would ask you to consider yourself at the whist table," he said in a low, confiding tone. "Trust there is a method to what may appear to be my madness."

"Eh?" Lady Clymore blinked at him, but Charles pressed a finger to his lips and drew away from her. Shifting her gaze to the cup hovering beneath her chin, her ladyship eyed it a moment, then put it down, untouched, as Iddings announced the Earl of Clymore.

Not surprisingly, Charles disliked him on sight. All gilt hair and fastidious dress, he looked the type to be affronted by the sight of an urchin in Berkeley Square, for there was no other reason for his lordship to cane the boy.

"Good evening, Julian," Lady Clymore said to him coolly. "Allow me to make you known to the Duke of Braxton."

Clearly he'd heard the name, for his brows fairly leapt off his head. "Your Grace," he said, with a stiff bow.

"Clymore." Charles acknowledged him with a brief nod—and made up his mind that the hackney driver who'd absconded with Boru was in the employ of Julian Dameron. It fit, both emotionally and rationally, that a man who would beat a child on a public street wouldn't hesitate to kidnap a dog. "Lady Clymore tells me you are newly arrived in town. Have you come on business or pleasure?"

"Mostly the former, Your Grace," he replied, seating himself on the companion settee grudgingly indicated by her ladyship, "but the Countess Featherston has been kind enough to include me in her invitations for tomorrow evening."

"I shall *kill* Clarissa," Lady Clymore muttered under her breath.

Julian's gaze cut briefly toward the countess, a thin smile not quite reaching his eyes. A memory of his father warning him never to sit down to cards with a man who smiled only with his mouth sprang to Charles's mind and hardened his resolve to uncover the upstart earl as Boru's kidnapper.

"What a happy coincidence," he drawled mildly. "I shall be escorting Lady Clymore and Betsy to the same affair."

Fortunately for Julian, he was squarely seated on the settee, else he might have toppled off it. *"Betsy?"* he repeated in a shocked voice.

"I'm sure you know her. Fairish, fetching little chit about so high." Charles lifted his right hand an inch or so above his head.

"Of course I *know* her. She's my cousin," Julian snapped affrontedly. "And her name is *Elizabeth*."

"To you, perhaps." Charles smiled benignly. "But then you are *distant* cousins, are you not?"

A sudden, bloodcurdling shriek and the drum of running feet echoed beyond the Blue Saloon. The crashing thud and excited, high-pitched barking that followed sent Charles and Julian racing for the closed doors and Lady Clymore struggling to her feet with her cane.

By half an arm's length, Charles beat Julian to the doors and flung them open. The urchin boy, clad only in dripping small clothes, lay kicking and screaming on the foyer floor with Betsy clinging to his knees. The little brown terrier snapped at the butler, who was trying to catch the boy's flailing arms, while a brawny footman with a towel hung about his neck tried to catch the dog.

"Elizabeth!" Julian thundered her name. "Get off the floor this instant!"

His voice, stinging like a whip with outrage and disapproval, brought instant silence from the boy and the terrier and obedience from Betsy. Snatching the cap that had slipped over her eyes off her head, she scrambled to her feet. Her skirts were streaked with wet spots, her sleeves rolled above the elbow. As her gaze shifted from Julian to Charles, her face scalded vermillion and her eyes lowered.

"Your Grace," she murmured, sinking—or rather, cringing, Charles thought—into a miserable curtsey. "My lord."

The boy took advantage of the billow her skirts made to grasp her hem, wrap it around himself, and cling to her legs. The little terrier whined and slinked beneath her petticoat. The servants froze like pillars.

"I must apologize for Elizabeth," Julian said curtly to Charles. "She is usually not *quite* so ramshackle in her behavior."

"Think nothing of it," Charles replied, with a dismissive wave. "I am becoming quite used to it, I assure you, and her behavior is nothing of the kind. Lady Elizabeth is acquitted to be quite an Original among the ton."

"I should think an *Unusual* or the veriest quiz would be more apt," Julian said darkly, as he started toward Betsy. "I cannot think what possessed you to bring this filthy brat into the house, Elizabeth, but I shall tend to him once and for all."

At that moment, Lady Clymore puffed her way painfully into the doorway beside Charles. "You will do *nothing* in *my house*, Dameron!"

"Must I remind you yet again, my lady," Julian challenged, spinning angrily toward her on one heel, "that *I* am head of this family now?"

"You may remind me until you turn blue in the face," Lady Clymore raged, shaking her cane at him, "but this is *my* house, upstart—entailed to me by my mother—and you have *no claim here*!"

While the dowager countess and the earl glared daggers at each other, Charles took quick stock of the situation. 'Twas a powder keg, to be sure, made worse by his presence, for he had no doubt Clymore was laying it on thick for his benefit. The boy quaked in obvious terror against Betsy's legs, despite the soothing hand his protectress laid upon his head. Charles spared a glance at Betsy, saw her free hand tighten into a fist against her skirts, and decided that grilling the Earl of Clymore about Boru would have to wait.

"Oh, bother, Lady Clymore." He took her elbow in one hand, snatched the cane in the other, and tossed it to Julian. "Let him be done with it."

He at least had the decency to flush to the roots of his gilt hair as he caught it. Otherwise, he stood staring mutely at Charles, his expression a mingle of anger, fury, and humiliation.

"Go on, Clymore," Charles urged him. "Finish the job. Beat the boy senseless."

A pitiful mewl escaped the child. From the corner of his eye, Charles saw him lift his face pleadingly to Betsy. Her fingers stroked his hair reassuringly and she murmured something to him Charles couldn't hear.

"You misunderstand, Your Grace," Julian said tightly. "I caught the wretch begging before the gates this morning."

"Beggary is not a crime, Clymore, it is an affliction. One which you apparently share."

Julian stiffened. "I do not know what you mean."

"I do not refer to the state of your finances, though it is common enough knowledge in the clubs," Charles lied, with an ease Teddy would have admired, for he hadn't been near any of his clubs in days. "I refer to your beggared spirit and *your* behavior before the gates this morning."

A fresh wash of color darkened Julian's face to a near-purple hue. Charles waited, expecting a glove across the cheek at any second. The prospect sent his blood singing with a vigor that mere hours ago would have alarmed him, but now he relished it, along with the pulse starting in his head again.

Julian's reaction was to clench Lady Clymore's cane more tightly in both hands. "Is protecting your kinswomen from riffraff no longer the fashion, Your Grace?"

"Riffraff, my foot!" Betsy took a challenging step forward with the boy clinging to her skirts. "We saw you turn Claxton away. You were protecting what you *mistakenly* consider to be your claim here."

Julian swung angrily about to face her. "I will remind you for the last time that *I* am head of this family!"

"So you may be," Betsy retorted, "but you have no power over me, for *I* choose not to grant you any."

The pride and disdain ringing in her voice drew an admiring grin from Charles and a choking sound from Julian.

"You choose *nothing* without my permission," he growled at her furiously.

"I'm afraid that's not entirely true, Clymore," Charles put in mildly, "for Betsy has chosen me."

Lady Clymore made a noise in her throat that was either dread or delight. Charles wasn't sure which, but there was no mistaking the soundless gasp of horror that parted Betsy's lips and widened her eyes, for it was a near twin to the expression on the earl's face as he swung abruptly about, her ladyship's cane slipping from his fingers and clattering to the floor. It was there for only a second, along with a flicker of something—perhaps panic, possibly rage, but more than likely desperation—that vanished when he squared his shoulders.

"We must speak privately, Your Grace, for I fear you have been misled."

"*You* have been misled, Clymore, by your own arrogance in thinking any person of breeding would allow you to force Lady Elizabeth to marry you just to save your sinking ship."

"You are misled again, Your Grace." A gleam of perspiration, despite the evening frost gathering in whorls on the foyer windows, gleamed on Julian's upper lip. "I hold Lady Eliz—er, Betsy, in the highest regard, and she—"

"Loathes the sight of you," Betsy cut in icily.

Lady Clymore clapped a hand to her brow and sagged against the doorframe. Julian, however, rounded on Betsy.

"*Clymore.*" The voice that had moved Teddy to prayer spun him back to Charles. "Now *you* have a choice. Either wish your cousin happy—or accept the loan of my glove."

Betsy went pale, bit her lip, and clung to the boy. Lady Clymore's hand shot from her brow to her mouth. The servants flinched, and the Earl of Clymore, his face nearly as white as Betsy's, shook violently with suppressed fury for a long moment.

"I wish you happy," he said at last between gritted teeth, then wheeled away to collect his hat, his stick, and his gloves. "I bid you all good evening."

With a curt bow, Julian made for the door. Iddings bestirred himself to open it and shut it behind him. Then he collected her ladyship's cane and returned it to her.

"Have you run mad, Braxton?" She rounded incredulously on Charles. "I thought the plan was to ascertain Dameron's involvement in Boru's disappearance, not to infuriate him and drive him beyond reason."

"It still is, my lady." Glimpsing Betsy staring woodenly at him, he stepped past the countess to reach the window and lift the drapery in time to see Julian ascend a hackney waiting just outside the gates.

When the coach rolled away, Charles moved hastily to the door with Lady Clymore's cane tapping behind him. Over his shoulder, he saw Betsy kneel to wrap the towel handed her by the footman around the boy, then rise to trail curiously but hesitantly behind her grandmother. Charles opened the door, plucked a handkerchief from his pocket, and waved it thrice in an arc above his head.

A moment later, another hackney rolled into view.

"What the devil—?" her ladyship muttered.

Smiling slyly, Charles tucked his handkerchief in his waistcoat. "Clymore is not the only one with a jarvey in his employ."

When the hackney drew parallel with the gates, Teddy's head popped out the window. "We're on him, Chas!" he shouted, the broad grin on his face gleaming in the flicker of the sidelamps.

At the ring of his voice across the courtyard, the driver, heavily swathed in dark greatcoat and pulled-down hat, turned in his box and thumped Lord Theodore on the head with the handle of his whip.

"My, my." Lady Clymore clucked admiringly. "Wherever did you find such an excellent coachman?"

"My brother Lesley." Charles watched Teddy rub his head and duck inside the hackney. Then he shut the door and moved to the window with the countess for a last glimpse of the coach bowling smartly but discreetly away in pursuit of Julian. "Member of the Four-in-Hand Club."

"Stout-looking whip," Lady Clymore observed. "Tell me Lord Lesley intends to thrash Boru's whereabouts out of Dameron and I shall be the happiest of females."

Charles laughed, but Betsy did not. Standing a step or so behind her grandmother, her hands clasped at her back, her gaze grave, almost reproachful, she looked the somberest of females. She

157

also looked among the loveliest with damp tendrils of hair curling about her ears. When she realized Charles was looking at her, she glanced at the floor.

"A delightful thought, but excessively bad form, I fear." Reluctantly he shifted his gaze from Betsy to the countess. "Lesley and Teddy will haunt Dameron and his rooms, follow wherever he goes, intercept any messages he might send or might be sent to him, until such time as Boru is safely returned to Berkeley Square."

Betsy raised just her eyes to his face. "Thank you, Your Grace. You are truly wonderful."

Charles didn't feel wonderful. He felt guilty and woefully undeserving of the gratitude shimmering in her gaze. "I would be honored if you would call me Charles," he said gently.

But Betsy only bit her lip and ducked her head again.

"As to that"—Lady Clymore thumped her cane against the floor and drew herself regally straight— "you do us a great honor and a gallant service by offering for Betsy. Once Dameron has taken himself and his odious attentions elsewhere, I shall not hold you to it, Braxton."

"But, my lady," Charles told her, with his most charming smile, "I most sincerely want you to."

So great was Lady Clymore's shock that if not for her cane and the steadying hand Charles hastily cupped around her elbow, she might have toppled over. "*You do?*"

"Yes, my lady, I—" Charles grinned suddenly. "Never mind. I shall save that phrase for the wedding."

Chapter Sixteen

"There will be no wedding," Betsy said, the very quietness of her voice doing more than a shout to underscore her resolve.

Charles did not miss it, but Lady Clymore did, for she made a quarter turn upon her cane and eyed her granddaughter as if she'd just sprouted another head. "What do you mean there will be no wedding? Of course there will. Braxton has offered for you."

"I have not accepted him, Granmama." Betsy addressed herself exclusively and adamantly to the countess. "And I have no intention of doing so."

"Of course you will! Have you lost your wits?"

"No, Granmama. *I* have not." Betsy speared Charles with a pointedly brief look. "I realize I must save myself from Julian and have formed a plan to do so."

"Indeed you have, miss," Lady Clymore retorted forcefully. "The plan is that you will marry Braxton."

"*No*, Granmama," Betsy replied emphatically. "I will not be dictated to—by *you* or Julian or *anyone* else. I have control of my own destiny, and, according to Papa's will, control of my fortune. It is mine to do with as I please."

"You impertinent, disrespectful chit!" Lady Clymore shrilled, with a thump of her cane.

"I do not mean to be, Granmama, I mean only to be my own person. I have been confused and frightened, but am determined to be no longer." Betsy's voice broke and began to quaver. "I have been devious, as well, and my deceptions have cost me Boru."

"You will have him back," Charles put in feelingly. "If it's the last thing I ever do, I'll find him for you."

"I think not, Your Grace." Betsy drew a breath and continued. "I have made an oath on Boru's memory to take myself back to Clymore. To the dower house, which is not entailed to Julian, where I will open a home for orphans."

"And where will I live, goose?"

"You have this house," Betsy reminded her grandmother, "and I will keep an apartment for you at Clymore, where you will be welcome whenever you wish to take the country air."

"You are overset," Lady Clymore informed her, and turned on her cane to smile at Charles. "Pay her no mind." Then her ladyship cocked a stern eyebrow at Iddings. "What is this boy doing dripping puddles on my floor?"

"This is Davey." Betsy stepped squarely into her grandmother's line of vision. "And I am not overset."

"Then you have run mad—and will make Braxton an excellent duchess!" Lady Clymore shook her cane threateningly. "Now take yourself off and change your gown before I beat some sense into you!"

Clutching the towel to his throat, the boy mewled

again and swooned. Charles saw him crumple and dashed forward to catch him before he hit the floor. Dropping to his knees, he cradled the frail little form in his arms and felt his throat tighten at the sight of his protruding ribs.

"Now see what you've done!" Betsy rushed to Charles's side, the little terrier whimpering at her heels. The hand she raised to Davey's pale forehead shook visibly. "Is he—?" She bit her lip, unable to finish.

"He has merely fainted." Charles rose with the boy in his arms. "You should have fed him before you tried to bathe him. I assume that's why he's wet to the skin."

"Y-yes," Betsy admitted haltingly. "He kicked up an awful dust about the bath, you see. I—I tried to bribe him into the tub with a pastry."

"I fear you have much to learn about orphans." Charles chided her with a gentle smile and glanced a nod at the archway. "I trust the kitchen is through there?"

"Yes, Your Grace."

"I'll take 'im, Yer Grace," George said, stepping forward and holding out his arms.

"Kind of you," Charles said, declining, "but he weighs hardly anything."

"This way, then, Your Grace." Iddings sprang quickly ahead to lead the way.

Her lips parted in amazement, Betsy scooped up Scraps and trailed the butler, Charles, and George through the archway. Clearly she had just as much to learn about dukes as she did about orphans.

"Have your wits gone begging?" Lady Clymore screeched. When no one replied, she howled, "Then may the orphans take you all!"

By the time they reached the kitchen Davey had roused from his swoon, but Cook nearly fell into one at the sight of Quality invading her domain. She went rigid as the spit she turned and spots of color as bright as the flames dancing in her hearth burned in her ample cheeks.

" 'Ello again, guv," Davey said, blinking and lifting his head from Charles's shoulder.

"Hello, Davey. How d'you feel?"

"Bit on th' rum side."

"Have a sit, then." Charles propped the boy in a wooden chair at Cook's scrubbed top table and gave her a courteous bow. "Good evening, ma'am. Might you have a meat pie or two for the lad?"

"I've this whole joint, m'lord," Cook offered generously, "which *her* don't need with her gouty foot."

"You are too kind," Charles replied, smothering a grin. "But I think a meat pie would be just the thing. What say you, Davey?"

"Lovely . . ." The boy sighed, his eyes glistening.

While Cook scrambled to fill the duke's request, Betsy fetched the scrap bowl usually saved for Boru. She put it down on the floor for the little terrier, rose, and watched Charles strip off his coat, help Davey into it, and roll the sleeves. With the towel, Charles dried the boy's hair, then swung a chair backward to the table and set down before Davey a platter full of beef and sausage pies, a pudding sprinkled with cinnamon, a plate of cheese and fruit, and a crock of Cook's own cider.

"S'all this fer me?" Davey asked, raising just his eyes from the table.

"I should say not." Charles took a fat pie, a large bite, and began to chew.

Wriggling forward, Davey did the same. His bare

ankles hooked together, his feet swinging against the rungs, he grinned at Charles with an overfull mouth.

"Rov'ry," he said.

Charles swallowed and grinned back at him. "Lovely, indeed." Then he poured the boy a cup full of cider.

Leaning forward to scratch Scraps behind the ears while he ate, Betsy sank onto the bench before the hearth. George brought a bowl of water for the dog, placed it carefully on the floor without spilling a drop, then donned his livery and gave himself over to Cook and Iddings and the task of serving Lady Clymore her supper.

The rapt expression on Betsy's face while she watched Davey eat and the fire gleaming on her hair made swallowing difficult for Charles. A swig of cider helped, but not much. Bending his elbows on the table, he chanced a glance at her. When she didn't look away, he smiled. She returned it tentatively.

"You seem much at home among pots and pans."

"I often dine with the servants at the hall." Charles took an orange and began to peel it. "The kitchen's much warmer and so is the company."

"Do you not entertain?"

" 'Tis difficult without a hostess," Charles said, and cursed himself when Betsy ducked her head. "I manage a little when my mother is in residence, or whenever Lady Cromley can lend a hand."

Betsy's gaze lifted, just a bit too quickly for casual curiosity. "Lady Cromley?"

"My widowed neighbor. Her late husband's estate marches with the hall."

She smiled again, not quite so tentatively, show-

163

ing a dimple in her left cheek Charles had never noticed before. The sight of it made him throb, break the orange apart, and offer her a section. She took it, popped it in her mouth, and pulled the bench closer to the table.

"How is it you know so much about orphans?"

"They abound in the country as well as the city. Caro—er, Lady Cromley, does what she can for them."

He offered another piece of orange, which Betsy accepted readily. When she licked juice from her fingertips, Charles smothered a groan of longing.

"Your plan," he said, his voice a bit deeper than usual, "seems well thought out but for one not so small detail. You can't possibly believe Dameron will abandon his pursuit of you merely because you wish to devote your life to saving orphans."

"For that reason alone, no. But when I offer him a generous quarterly allowance, yes." Betsy gave him a shyly sly smile. "I wish I'd thought of it at Clymore, for we need never have come to town at all."

"Do you not like London?"

"I do not. I love the country. But I was so unhappy when Papa died, and in such a panic when Julian began hectoring me, I allowed Granmama to convince me that throwing myself on the marriage mart was my only hope."

She said no more, but her thinking was clear to Charles: If she'd stayed at Clymore, she would still have Boru.

"Your plan is clever but costly. I have a cheaper one."

A wary gleam came into Betsy's eyes. "What is that?"

"Not what you think. I am not Dameron. I do not force unwilling females into marriage."

"But I didn't mean—" she began, flushing and lowering her eyes when Charles cocked an eyebrow. "Yes, I *did* mean, and I apologize." Betsy looked up at him. "You were saying, Your Grace?"

"I do wish you would call me Braxton," Charles said exasperatedly. "My lord, if you must, but anything, please, save Your Grace. It makes me feel the veriest antique."

Betsy eyed him consideringly for a moment, then said, "As you wish, my lord."

She was still wary, still not quite at ease with him. After the way he'd behaved in Hyde Park, Charles didn't blame her. As one offers a tidbit to a dog to gain its trust—an insulting analogy but the first that came to mind—Charles offered her the last orange slice.

"I was saying that so long as Dameron thinks we are betrothed he will be forced to look elsewhere for an heiress."

"And you truly think he believes your offer?"

The dubious tone of her voice made it clear that she did not. Not yet, at any rate. But by heaven, Charles vowed, she would. And he would know if she truly cared for him.

"I do, and am certain that whatever doubts he might have will vanish once he reads the announcement in the *Times.*"

Betsy swallowed hard, the orange thudding like a rock into her stomach. "What announcement?"

"Why, the announcement of our engagement, of course."

"I should have *known*!" Betsy shot to her feet.

"Kindly allow me to finish," Charles retorted,

springing out of his chair. "I merely propose we maintain the facade until Clymore finds himself another fortune. Then you may cry off with no harm done."

Betsy's eyes widened incredulously. *"No harm done!"*

"Not a whit's worth. Engagements are made to be broken. Why, the newspapers are full of retractions. Everyone will think you have merely come to your senses, that is all, for half the ton already believes me to be as dotty as His Poor Majesty."

"I should have known," Betsy repeated, her voice quavering and tinged with bitterness.

The unshed tears shimmering in her eyes gave Charles an almost physical pain, but he held resolutely to his course. "What should you have known?"

"That it was all a hum," Betsy retorted quickly, realizing—Praise God—that she'd come dangerously close to revealing her true feelings. "Which I knew, of course."

The hollow laugh she gave didn't fool Charles, rather it exhilarated him. Nearly to the point that he scooped her up in his arms, but mindful of Davey's avidly upturned face, he restrained himself. She deserved wooing, did this gentle, kind-hearted Aphrodite, and she would have it. Beginning tomorrow night at the Countess Featherston's ball.

"I am glad you were not deceived," he replied. "Pity Lady Clymore was, but there's nothing for it now."

"You were quite brilliant, my lord." Betsy forced her shaky knees to bend, and once she was reseated on the bench, forced her brightest smile. "I nearly believed you myself."

166

"Ah, but you are far too intelligent to be so easily gulled. Which, of course, *I* recognized the instant I read the note you enclosed with my coat."

If he'd called her Aphrodite again Betsy couldn't have been more stricken—or more grateful that she was sitting down. "I fear I must apologize for that, as well. At the time I was rather vexed with you, my lord."

"You had every reason to be, just as I did to be vexed with you at Lady Pinchon's rout."

"I knew that you were, but I still have no idea why."

"It was silly of me to believe him—I see that now and admit it freely—but just that afternoon Teddy had told me he planned to elope with you to Gretna."

"Yes, I know." Betsy felt herself flush and hoped Charles would acquit it to her proximity to the fire. "But did he explain to you why?"

"Yes, after I threatened to choke him."

From the corner of his eye, Charles saw Davey's jaws stop working. Making a note to omit any references to physical violence from his conversation when in the boy's presence, he shot him a hasty but warm smile.

"That is merely a figure of speech, Davey. Teddy is my youngest brother. I would never really choke him."

But I might, Betsy thought vengefully, imagining the fists clenched in her lap around Teddy's throat.

"Teddy's confession gave me the idea of telling Dameron we'd come to an understanding in the first place," Charles said sincerely. "In the second, it seemed the very least I could do to make amends for causing you to lose Boru."

"*You* are not responsible, my lord, *I* am," Betsy countered swiftly. "It was my idea to use Boru to chase Julian away. I placed him in jeopardy and I—I will have to live with that the rest of my life."

Then she caught her lip between her teeth and lowered her chin again. Where the firelight touched her hair it shimmered like molten gold.

"I believe we are both at fault for things beyond the loss of Boru," Charles said gently, "and it is my most sincere wish that we begin our acquaintanceship anew."

Her chin shot up, just a hair too quickly for his liking. "To what end?"

"I wish nothing more than to be your friend," Charles told her. At least for the moment, he added to himself.

"I would like that," Betsy told him, her eyes shining, "and would be honored to call you my friend."

"My friends," Charles shot back, with a grin, "call me Braxton."

"Touché, my lord," Betsy responded, laughing at last.

"'Ow come y'got s'many names, guv?" Davey asked.

"It's a long story," Charles said, shifting in his chair to look at the boy. "One I would be delighted to tell you while you have your bath."

"Already 'ad one," he said, glaring unhappily at Betsy.

"Ah, but did your furry little friend?"

"Why's Scraps need a bath?"

"Fleas, my boy. Scraps, I'm sure, would not wish to share his with Boru."

" 'E don' 'ave fleas. I picks 'em off."

"Then you must have them, too," Charles replied, sliding Betsy a sidelong glance, "and you wouldn't want to give them to Lady Betsy, would you?"

Picking up on his cue, Betsy stiffened suddenly on the bench. "Oh, my!" she exclaimed, scratching her shoulder.

"Too late," Charles intoned ominously, trapping Davey in a steady stare.

"Will a bath git rid 'o 'em?"

"I believe so, yes," Charles assured him. "And I believe Scraps would take to the water much better if you were to climb in with him."

"Figgered you'd say that." Davey sighed resignedly.

Chapter Seventeen

Once Lady Clymore had been served dessert, George and Iddings returned to the kitchen, shed their coats, and heated more water. Dragging the hip bath before the fire, they filled it and stepped back. Teeth gritted and eyes squinted, Davey clutched Scraps in his thin arms and climbed into the tub.

Rolling up his sleeves, Charles went down on his knees and took up a cloth and soap. While he scoured the boy from stem to stern, he told him all the titles he held and how he'd come by them.

The list was rather long, sufficiently so that Charles had to stop and think and correct it twice. Listening to him, elbow deep in murky water, scrubbing grime and coal dust from Scraps's shaggy coat (the blister on her hand stinging just a little), Betsy felt her heart swell and tears prick her eyes.

How kind and patient Charles was, how handsome with his hair burnished copper by the fire and water gleaming like quicksilver on his muscled forearms. There was nothing of the lunatic about him now, or the tyrant he'd been at Lady Pinchon's. How ridiculously and hopelessly in love with him she was, for he wished only to be her friend.

And how fervently Betsy hoped he wouldn't remember that he'd kissed her twice this day, for if his memory of *all* the events in Hyde Park returned he would, as a gentleman, feel bound by honor to marry her. He remembered Boru disappearing, but had made no mention of anything else, which she took as a hopeful sign. For no matter how friendly his feelings toward her, Betsy wouldn't—*couldn't*—marry him without at least a glimmer of the fevered gleam she'd seen earlier in his eyes.

Though it had frightened her and she'd mistaken it for madness induced by his fall, she longed to see at least a spark of it now in his blue-green eyes, for it had occurred to her that love was not unlike madness. There was no discernible logic to it, and precious little reason, for it made no sense at all that the mere sight of this man, who'd been less than kind to her in most of their encounters, should leave her feeling so breathless. Still, it did, and it saddened her, too, when the wink he gave her, as Davey rose from the water with chattering teeth, held only amusement and a conspiratorial twinkle.

Wrapping the boy in one towel and Scraps in another, Betsy sat on the bench with the terrier on her lap to dry him, while Charles carried Davey off to the scullery to dress him in brown breeches, a white shirt, and a blue vest borrowed from the pot boy. When he returned, leading a shy and transformed Davey with shiny and still-damp blond hair by the hand, the smile on the duke's face glowed with almost paternal pride.

"How handsome you are!" Betsy exclaimed to Davey, unwrapping the little dog from the towel and holding him up for all to admire. "And look at Scraps!"

His coat was no longer shaggy but silky, a mix

of tan and chocolate brown. He wiggled and whimpered happily in Betsy's hands, until a vividly blushing Davey took the little dog in his arms, cuddled him to his chest, and burst into sobs.

Blinking madly at the tears swimming in her eyes, Betsy bowed her head and bit her lip. She started, just a bit, when Charles sidled up beside her and laid a hand gently on her shoulder.

"You are learning, my lady," he murmured to her.

"Thanks to you," Betsy said softly, looking up at him over her shoulder.

The tears glistening like tiny diamonds on her lashes held Charles enthralled until Davey, with a loud, watery sniffle, dragged a sleeve across his nose and looked up at them. His face was still flushed from his scrubbing, but smudges of fatigue were beginning to show beneath his eyes.

"Long day, eh, Davey?"

He yawned and knuckled his eyes. "Bit o' one, guv."

"Then off to bed with you." Betsy rose from the bench and held out a hand to him.

When his fingers, still cool and puckered from his bath, slid trustingly around hers, Betsy bit back another well of tears. "George's room is just off the kitchen," she explained, "and he has kindly put up a cot for you there."

This was Charles's suggestion, made while he'd washed Davey's hair and the boy had screeched like a banshee.

"Yer th' one tried t'catch Boru," the boy said, turning his head to look at George.

"Roight—er, right, I am," George replied, with a

sheepish but encouraging smile. "Ye c'n help me stoke the fires come mornin' an' earn yer keep."

"Right w'me," Davey replied, his little chest swelling.

Pride was important, Charles had explained to Betsy over the boy's god-awful howls, and charity anathema. To young ladies of Quality as much as orphans, Betsy thought, aware of Charles trailing behind her as she and Davey followed George and the candle the footman picked up through the kitchen and into his small, spare room. He put it down on a tiny table near the cot and quietly withdrew to let Betsy tuck the boy into bed.

Folding his arms across his unbuttoned waistcoat and the soaked front of his shirt, Charles watched her help Davey shuck off his breeches, tug down his shirttails, and crawl beneath the covers. Most of the Little Season's debutantes would have swooned dead away at the sight of even a child in small clothes, but there wasn't so much as a hint of false modesty about Lady Betsy Keaton. What an interesting mix of capability and nonsense she was. Perhaps the fact that she loathed the city accounted for part of it, Charles thought, and what a delightful time he was going to have discovering the others.

"Should I leave the candle?" Betsy asked, tucking the turned-down sheet and blanket beneath Davey's chin.

"N-no," he replied, his gaze sliding toward Scraps, sitting obediently with ears pricked beside the bed.

Betsy scooped up the dog with a smile and plopped him onto Davey's stomach. His tail wagging happily, Scraps licked her fingers, then stretched out on his master's chest and tucked his nose under his chin. Wrapping his arms around his dog, Davey regarded Betsy gravely.

"T'morrow, after we 'elp George do th' fires," he said, "me an' Scraps'll go look fer Boru."

"You'll do no such thing," Betsy countered firmly. "He'll find his way home, don't you worry."

"But I seen that there jarvey take 'im up. 'E can't find 'is way 'ome tied up in ropes."

" 'Tied up'?" Betsy repeated faintly, lifting a hand to her throat.

"Who tied him up?" Charles asked, quickly stepping closer to the cot.

"Th' jarvey, o'course." Davey shifted his gaze to Charles. "Got down from 'is box wi'a rope an' whistled. When Boru come close, 'e grabbed his collar, put one end o' th' rope round 'is neck, t'other round 'is feet, and then round 'is mouth, I giss so's 'e couldn't bite. That's when th' man wi' th' cane got out and heped 'im lift Boru inside."

"Julian!" Betsy's hand slid away from her throat. "Do you mean the man who was here earlier?"

Davey nodded solemnly.

"I'll tie *him* up in ropes!" Betsy shot off the cot— straight into Charles's outstretched hands. There was no fear in her eyes at his touch, only fury. "Let me pass, my lord. I must find Boru."

"Indeed we must, my dear, but where do we look? You do not know his direction, and neither will I until I reconnoiter with Lesley and Teddy later this evening."

"Oh, that's right." Betsy sighed disappointedly and stepped back out of his grasp.

"Will you see me out?"

"Yes, of course." Betsy slipped her hand around

174

the arm Charles offered and was led briefly back to
the cot. "Would you recognize this jarvey if you see
him again, Davey?"

"That I would, guv."

"Then you shall help us find Boru." Charles
leaned forward to blow out the candle and tousle
the boy's hair. "But for now you must rest and be
fresh for the search on the morrow."

"Aye, guv." Davey sighed and rolled on his side,
tucking Scraps in the curve of his body.

"Good night," Betsy bid him softly, but his eyes
were already drifting shut, his lashes casting shadows on his cheeks in the half light spilling through
the door.

"Damn and blast," Charles said when they
reached the kitchen. "I wish now I hadn't lost my
temper with Dameron, and that I'd questioned Davey more closely in the park."

So much, he thought, for Teddy's theory that Davey would have mentioned Julian if he'd seen him.

"I should have let Granmama shoot him." Betsy
frowned angrily, unrolled the sleeves of his coat,
and handed the garment to him. "I may, in fact,
shoot him myself."

"Not with the pistol you carry in your reticule."

"Pistol?" she blinked at him blankly.

"You must recall it," Charles replied, with equal
innocence. "It's the one you carry in your reticule
merely for the effect."

"Oh," Betsy groaned more than said. "*That* pistol." Then she flushed to the roots of her hair.

"The very one," Charles confirmed, holding her
gaze steadily in his. "Teddy explained it had been
disabled."

"You . . . found my reticule?" she asked haltingly.

"And everything in it," Charles replied, shrugging into his coat with a pointedly arched eyebrow.

When she'd discovered her reticule missing, Betsy had hoped—no, *prayed*—that she'd lost it or a footpad had stolen it from the park. Knowing now that Charles had found it and all its contents, she wished the floor would open and swallow her.

"It's in my carriage," Charles told her. "I'll fetch it for you."

"Please don't. I never want to see it again." Spreading her fingers over her eyes, Betsy peeked through them. "You must think me the most ramshackle female ever born."

"On the contrary." He straightened his lapels and took her wrists lightly in his hands. "I quite agree with the ton. You are *definitely* an Original."

His smile and glint in his eyes—mischief, not madness or passion, but a glint nonetheless—made Betsy laugh. Shakily, for the graze of his thumbs on the backs of her hands rendered breathing difficult.

"Spanish coin, sir."

"Not a bit of it. I am merely delighted that we are now on friendly footing." Charles deepened his smile, and was not surprised when Betsy's eyes darted away from him. "You need not look about for something to smash me with, Betsy, dear, for I am quite recovered from my clout on the head."

When her gaze shifted hesitantly back to him, she smiled. "You see, I even know who you are."

"I did not mean to imply that you are insane, my lord, merely—addled. Temporarily, of course," Betsy added hastily.

How much did he remember? she wondered, her heart beginning to pound fast and frantic. Please not everything—oh, please not that he'd kissed her.

"You would not be the first to think me a lunatic," Charles admitted, "for I have made something of a career out of pretending to be one."

"But why, my lord?"

"It was a means to an end, which I shall explain to you tomorrow evening. I told Dameron, by the way, that I am escorting you and Lady Clymore, and so I will." Reluctantly Charles loosed her hands. "I shall call for you at nine of the clock. Until then."

He made her a small bow, touched a finger lightly to his lips and then to her chin, and strode out of the kitchen. The tenderness of the gesture sent Betsy floating up to her bedchamber, wondering the whole way if it was at all possible that Charles cared for her just a little.

After ringing for her abigail, she darted to the window, which faced the front of the house and gave her a view of the courtyard and Charles striding toward his carriage. At the shimmer of the coach lamps on the dark shoulders of his coat, she raised her fingertips to her chin and watched him mount the steps Fletcher had placed.

Neither Betsy nor George, who scurried out of the house to shut the gates behind the departing carriage, saw the two dark shapes detach themselves from the shadows at the mouth of the square.

"I told you," the jarvey said to Julian, in a low, testy tone in the rattling wake of Charles's coach, "I *told* you th' two coves who followed us wouldn't dare come back 'ere t'report I'd lost 'em."

"So you did, Owens," Julian replied implacably. "Still, it never hurts to make sure."

"I don't see why," the jarvey grumbled, hunkering down in his greatcoat with a shiver. "Don't see what diff'ernce it makes who does the followin'."

"But it does, Owens, for if it was Lady Clymore who was onto me—and I know now that it isn't—I would have had to alter my plans."

"Which 'ad better include," Owens said darkly, "payin' me fer catchin' an' keepin' that whackin' great hound."

"It does, rest assured." Julian laid a hand on the jarvey's shoulder. "With a little extra for your trouble."

And his own, which now included avenging the insult handed him by the Duke of Braxton—as well as seeing a period put to his offer for Betsy. He intended to accomplish them both, in one gloriously fell swoop, with just a bit more assistance from the surly jarvey.

"'Ow much more?" Owens asked, his small, close-set eyes gleaming with avarice in the darkness.

Julian named a figure that made the jarvey's eyes positively glow. "Wha'do I 'ave t'do fer it?"

"Nothing much." Julian smiled. "Simply rent a better carriage for tomorrow evening, one with a larger boot, and make yourself available to drive me to a ball."

Chapter Eighteen

When Charles reached Bond Street, Lesley was in the library. Still in his greatcoat, the whip Lady Clymore had so admired thwacking against one boot, a thunderous expression on his face.

"The bounder gave me the slip," he blurted, rounding on Charles when he came through the door. "Knows the streets like the back of his hand, damn him to hell."

"So we've no idea," Charles summed up, "of Dameron's direction or Boru's whereabouts?"

"None," Lesley snapped angrily. "But I'll know the blackguard's cattle when I see 'em again, and I plan to be on the streets at first light."

"And I will be as well," Charles said, with a frown.

"No offense, Chas, but I think this business is best left to Teddy and I."

"None taken, for I meant that I would be on my way to Berkeley Square to gainsay Betsy."

And he was, at scarce ten of the clock the next morning, the headache that was fast becoming an old friend thudding in his temples. He sent a note ahead announcing his arrival and was ushered straight into the Blue Saloon by Iddings, where

Lady Clymore awaited him with the tea tray and Betsy.

Her heart, which had leapt with hope at receipt of his note, sank with her first glimpse of Charles's face. He looked handsome as ever, but unrested and harried.

"Unfortunately," he announced, once he'd seated himself, "the jarvey managed to escape Lesley last night. No easy task, but apparently he's a clever fellow."

"So we do not know Julian's direction," Betsy said, with a sigh of disappointment.

"I fear not, but Lesley and Teddy have resumed the hunt this morning."

"Then I shall join them," she said, rising resolutely from the settee.

"I strongly advise against it," Charles replied, getting to his feet with her. "Lesley is unknown to Dameron—and the jarvey, for that matter—while you, my lady, are not. And they are already wise to the fact that someone followed them last night."

Betsy thought about that for a moment. "Then I will disguise myself."

"I forbid it!"

It was the wrong thing to say, and Charles knew it even as he uttered the words. But it was too late, for Betsy was already rounding on him with flashing eyes.

"You have no power to forbid me *anything*, my lord."

"Forgive my poor choice of words, my lady," he apologized hastily. "But old habits are hard to break."

"Are you referring to your habit of ordering people about merely because you are a duke?"

"I have *never*," Charles snapped at her, the pain in his temples flaring, "ordered anyone about merely because I am a duke."

"Oh, I see." Betsy folded her arms and tapped the toe of one slipper. "Then you must be referring to your habit of ordering people about because you are a tyrant."

"I am *not* a tyrant!"

"Really?" Betsy's toe tapped faster. "Are you not shouting at me like one?"

"I am shouting," Charles replied, gritting his teeth to keep from doing so, "because I am angry, not because I am a tyrant."

"Are you not angry because I refuse to bend to your will?"

"Indeed not!" Charles gave up trying not to and shouted. "I am angry because you are behaving like a featherheaded little chit!"

"Featherheaded!" Betsy stamped her foot and shouted back at him. "How *dare* you!"

"Someone must to keep you from haring off dressed as God knows what and risking your own safety, not to mention that of Boru's!"

"As if you care!" Betsy retorted scathingly. "Since you cannot deny that just yesterday you were trying to throttle him!"

"The hell I was! I was merely trying to keep my feet!"

"Is that why your hands were around his throat?"

"If I'd intended to throttle him," Charles returned, striving to regain a measure of composure, "would I have enlisted Teddy and Lesley to search for him?"

"To ease your guilty conscience," Betsy shot back, "I believe you would do anything!"

"Then you must still believe the world is flat!"

"But not nearly so flat as your excuses, my lord!"

"Go on, then!" Charles gave an irritable wave of his hand. "Rig yourself out as a footman or a page and prove to Dameron and the rest of the ton that all the rackety things he says about you are true!"

It was an unkind remark—and the very thing he'd been trying to save her from. Charles could not believe he'd said it, pressed a hand to his splitting head, and watched her face harden into a mask of icy fury.

"Since my acquaintance with *you*, my lord, has given me such a vast knowledge of the animal," Betsy retorted viciously, "I believe I will disguise myself as a *goatherd*!"

"There are no goatherds in London!"

"Only *goats* masquerading as *dukes*!"

"Enough!" Lady Clymore got to her feet and thumped her cane. "Put a period to this *at once*, before you both say things you will regret!"

"I regret," Betsy seethed, "*only* that I allowed you to kiss me!"

"What?" Lady Clymore squawked, her gaze flying from Betsy to Charles and back again. "When was this?"

"You allowed *nothing*!" Charles shot back, ignoring the countess. "You nearly cracked my skull with that damned heavy volume of Ovid!"

"Who the blazes is Ovid?" her ladyship demanded.

"Come near me again," Betsy threatened, clenching her fist at Charles, "and I *will* crack your head!"

"Do so," he returned angrily, "and no one will believe we are engaged. Not even Dameron!"

"Good! For we are *not* and *never* will be!"

"The hell you say! I do *not* reneg on my word!"

"Liar!" Betsy shrilled at him. "Last eve you said you do not force unwilling females into marriage!"

"Rest assured, I have no intention of marrying you, but I *do* intend to keep my word, which is to maintain the facade until Dameron makes another match!"

"I do not need your assistance to rid myself of Julian!"

"Perhaps not, but you shall have it!"

"We shall see about *that*, *Your Grace!*" Betsy bobbed him a curtsey, snatched up her skirts, and flung herself toward the door.

Charles rounded on his heel to follow her, but stopped, stricken to the bone at the glimpse he had of her profile. Her lips quivered and unshed tears glistened on her lashes. It hit him then, much as her tiny fist had the day before, that what he'd taken for anger and loathing of him was perhaps guilt and hurt, the very feelings he was experiencing himself, more sharply and painfully than he'd ever felt anything before.

He'd been a fool again, an idiot, had let the banked fires let loose in him the day before, blaze unchecked. When the saloon door slammed shut behind Betsy, Charles sprang after her and reached the bottom step of the staircase just as she reached the landing.

"Betsy, wait—" he began, but she whirled on her heel, snatched up a vase resting on a shelf, and hurled it at him.

Flinging up an arm, Charles ducked and felt the

vase whiz past his head. When it exploded against the wall behind him, he raised his head, saw the empty landing, and a moment later heard the echoing slam of a door somewhere on the corridor above.

"If she'd been herself, she wouldn't have missed," Lady Clymore told him.

Sagging wearily against the banister on his left arm, Charles looked at the countess framed in the saloon doorway. Hands cupped on the head of her cane, she cocked her head to one side and arched an eyebrow at him.

"Would you do me the honor, Lady Clymore, of thrashing me with your cane?"

"Rest assured, Braxton, that if you don't think of a way to patch this up I most definitely will."

Charles bent his elbow and dragged his hand through his hair. "How do you know she didn't mean what she said?"

"That's the crux of the problem, you silly man. She doesn't believe you genuinely want to marry her. And why should she, when you just told her you didn't?"

"But that's not at all what I meant to say." Charles raised his hand and pinched the bridge of his nose. "It's this damnable headache."

"I'm sure you did not," Lady Clymore responded kindly, "anymore than Betsy meant to compare you to a goat."

"No, my lady." Charles lowered his hand and gave her a rueful glance. "I'm reasonably certain she meant that. The question is how do I convince her I'm not?"

"I cannot help you there. I can only do this." Lady Clymore moved to a nearby bellpull and gave it a tug.

A moment later, Iddings appeared. "Yes, my lady?"

"Lady Betsy is in her room. Lock her in and do not let her out, no matter what she threatens."

"As you wish, my lady." Iddings bowed and moved past Charles up the stairs.

"Thank you, ma'am," he said, with a sigh, turning and downing the step to the foyer. "That's one less thing I have to worry about."

"I suggest you do not escort us to the Countess Featherston's this evening. Betsy will not expect it after this, and in her present mood, I think it unwise to throw the two of you together in a closed carriage."

"I cannot, my lady, for I told Dameron—"

"Hang Dameron," Lady Clymore cut in. "Concentrate on redeeming yourself with Betsy and let me worry about getting her there."

"Very well, my lady. I bow to your superior wisdom." As he did over the hand she offered him, gritting his teeth against the sickening thud in his temples.

"I am not wise, Braxton, I am merely an old woman anxious to see her granddaughter settled." Her ladyship gave him a stern look when he straightened. "Make no mistake about that."

"Not for an instant, ma'am," Charles told her feelingly, certain that in the short space of time he'd known Betsy Keaton he'd already made enough mistakes for a lifetime.

A feeling of doom hung heavy on Charles's shoulders when he returned to Bond Street to dress for the evening, but it was no heavier or gloomier than the pall shrouding Betsy's heart. She'd spent the day so deep in the dismals that she hadn't even attempted to leave her bedchamber—and so had no idea the door was locked until she rang for her Abigail and she heard the key turn in Soames's hand.

"Who locked my door and *why*?" she demanded, springing to her feet from the bed when the maid entered.

"Her Ladyship, of course," Soames replied, "t'keep you from runnin' off lookin' fer Boru dressed like a shepherd."

"Goatherd," Betsy snapped, flinging herself down at her glass.

Her reflection showed her flushed cheeks and glittering, overbright eyes. She knew very good and well whose idea it was to lock her in, for her grandmother had never dared such a thing before. The tyrant. The arrogant, insufferable prig. The overbearing, high-in-the-instep Duke of Braxton.

She'd show *him*, Betsy vowed, giving her cheeks a good hard pinch to redden them even more. The Countess Featherston's ball was *the* event of the Little Season, the last great fete before the ton retired to the country for the shooting and holiday seasons. Only the crème de la crème received invitations, and Betsy was suddenly determined to outshine them all.

Just as determined as Julian Dameron was to ruin her once and for all. And by nine of the clock, the stage was set for it.

Lord and Lady Featherston's Grosvenor Square mansion was ablaze with torches, the streets were crammed with carriages, the steps leading to the house carpeted in green velvet and dotted with jewel-gowned debutantes like autumn leaves scattered across a lawn.

Behind a mother and two daughters, Julian made his way into the house, pleased to see over his shoulder that absolutely no one noticed Owens drive his team into the mews behind the square. No one but Davey, riding in the box of the Clymore coach with Silas and George, and he kept it to himself until Betsy and the countess were safely delivered to the door. Then he tugged George's sleeve and whispered in his ear.

A more perfect setting couldn't be had, Julian decided, for everyone who was anyone packed the saloons to overflowing. He recognized them all, for he'd taken Lady Clymore's advice and studied who was who (or was it whom?) among the beau monde. Carefully, he kept himself in the thick of the crush. Since being followed from Berkeley Square, he had no wish to be pinned in a corner by Charles. At the proper moment, yes, but not until then.

At length he reached the ballroom, awash in the glow of thousands of candles glittering among the crystal facets of several chandeliers. Already the flowers artfully arranged in tall Grecian vases and upon marble pedestals were beginning to droop in the heat.

Four pairs of French windows stood open to admit the cool night air. Just as Julian had known they would. Beyond the frothy panels billowing in the light breeze, the fairy lights strung around the garden twinkled like stars. Their reflections danced in Julian's eyes while he fetched himself a glass of champagne and drank it behind a tall screen of greenery, waiting and dreaming of the first ball he and Betsy would hold at Clymore.

Bending a palm frond or two gave him a view of the entrance and Lady Clymore arriving with

Betsy. The dowager had abandoned the cane she'd used the night before, which caused Julian only a moment's disappointment, for his mouth fell open at the sight of his cousin. At last he understood her appeal, for there wasn't a hint of the rackety hoyden he knew at Clymore in the bewitching creature gowned in spun-sugar pink dotted with pearls.

Julian's jaw was not the only one to come unhinged at the sight of Betsy, but Charles's was the only one to clench. Not in vexation but in pain, for the headache was pounding full force in his head and the glass of nauseatingly sweet punch he'd chosen was only making it worse. His drawn-together brows and an errant lock of hair gave him a satyric look that caused Julian to retreat further into the shrubbery when Charles stopped in front of him to flag down a footman and exchange his punch for champagne.

The duke's resemblance to the mythological creature was not lost on Betsy as he tossed off the contents of his glass, looked up, and met her gaze.

A jolt of awareness shot through her at the contact but she looked pointedly away and snapped open her fan. If only he weren't so handsome in his dark evening dress with his hair gleaming like a raven's wing. It would be so much easier to despise him.

From his vantage behind the palms, Julian watched Teddy converge on Betsy. He was not concerned with the puppy, however, only with Braxton, depositing his empty glass on a passing footman's tray and striking off to intercept Lady Clymore.

"You are a vision, my lady," Teddy told Betsy.

"Thank you," she muttered unhappily, observing

Charles's progress over the edge of her fan. "I'm glad *someone* notices. You can't imagine how long it takes to transform oneself into a vision."

Teddy slid his gaze in the direction Betsy looked and smiled. "I'm sure Chas has noticed. In fact, I'll wager he's remarking upon it to her ladyship even as we speak."

Fat chance, Betsy thought glumly, knowing she should stop staring at Charles. She couldn't seem to help herself, though, couldn't drag her gaze away or swallow the lump in her throat. When he bowed over Lady Clymore's hand and led her onto the floor for a waltz, Betsy thought she would burst into tears at the pink flush of pleasure staining her grandmother's cheeks.

"I'll wager," she snapped waspishly at Teddy, "that you are mistaken."

When he did not reply, she glanced sideways and saw him staring, slack-jawed and wide-eyed, at a point on the opposite side of the ballroom. Betsy craned her neck, but could not see Julian or anyone else she knew.

"Whatever are you looking at?"

"Not *what*, *who*," Teddy replied woodenly.

"Well, who then?" Or was it *whom*, Betsy wondered, but couldn't decide.

"Lady Caroline Cromley," he announced gravely.

"Your country neighbor. Marvelous." Betsy brightened at the recollection of Charles telling her Lady Cromley did what she could for orphans in the parish. "Where is she?"

With a tight-lipped nod, Teddy indicated a tall, handsome woman with chestnut hair piled in intricate curls atop her head. The picture she made, her fulsome figure gowned in saffron silk, amethysts at her throat and on her fingers, clashed with the image of dowdiness Charles had left in her head. He'd never said she *wasn't* a great beauty, still it was hard to picture this regal creature wrestling dirty children or scrubbing their hair. Picturing her performing either task with Charles gave Betsy an uncomfortable stab.

"She's—quite lovely," she said haltingly.

"The loveliest widow in the entire parish." Teddy spread his fingers over his eyes. "Chas will kill me."

"Don't be silly. He'll be as delighted to see her as I will be to make her acquaintance." Betsy closed her fan and draped it over her wrist. "Introduce me, Teddy. Lady Cromley and I have much to discuss."

"I'm sure you do," he replied, catching her arm as she started forward, "but this is not the time or the place."

Betsy cocked her head at him puzzledly. "To discuss orphans?"

"Oh ... the orphans!" Teddy laughed giddily with relief. "I thought perhaps you wanted to scratch her eyes out."

"Why on earth would I—?" Betsy's breath caught in her throat as realization dawned. Charles called her Caro ... and she was the loveliest widow in all the parish. What a fool she was. No wonder Charles had no wish to marry her. "Why is he going to kill you?"

"Because I forged a note in his hand inviting Lady Cromley to London."

"Teddy!" Betsy rounded on him, aghast. "How *could* you?"

"It seemed a good idea at the time," he admitted sheepishly. "But then I forgot I'd done it."

"If Charles doesn't kill you," Betsy threatened, backing him into a close-by corner with her folded fan, "I *will*."

Chapter Nineteen

Suicide, not murder, was the first thought to leap into Charles's head when he glimpsed Caroline Cromley. So stunned was he that he missed the next step and trod upon Lady Clymore's gouty foot.

"God's teeth!" she howled, in a voice that nearly drowned out the orchestra.

A good portion of the guests heard her. Some twittered, one or two moved to help Charles and the countess crumpling in pain against his arm. Among them was Betsy, her eyes glittering. With anger or unshed tears Charles couldn't tell.

"My lady, I'm so terribly sorry," he apologized, helping Lady Clymore limp off the dance floor.

"Not your fault," she said, wincing with each halting step she took. "It's this demmed foot."

Watching Betsy draw to a halt on the near sidelines, Charles wondered why he had the feeling she already knew who Caroline was. Then he caught sight of Teddy making his way toward them through the crowd and wondered no more.

"Come with me, Granmama." Betsy held her hands out to take charge of the dowager. "I shall take you home."

"The devil you will. Finish this waltz with Braxton."

"I'd rather not," Betsy replied distastefully, "but I'm sure Lady Cromley would be delighted."

"Lady who?" The countess blinked curiously.

"My *neighbor* at the hall," Charles replied, emphatically and solely for Betsy's benefit.

"The loveliest widow in all the parish." She addressed herself to her grandmother, but gave him a reproachful glare. "A great expert on orphans."

"Excellent." Lady Clymore stepped out of Charles's embrace and into Betsy's. "Then perhaps she'll take that noisome boy off our hands."

"I believe she already has, Granmama." Betsy leveled a contemptuous look on Charles, then turned her back on him to put an arm around her grandmother and lead her away.

Charles would have gone after her, but a hand settled gently on his sleeve and he turned around. All thoughts of choking, kissing, or merely shouting at Betsy vanished at the sight of Caroline Cromley, and so did the peal he thought to ring over her when she withdrew a letter from her reticule. He recognized the script and asked puzzledly, "When did I write that to you, Caro?"

"You didn't," she replied, handing him the letter. "I don't know who did, but I thought you should know someone is impersonating you. It's why I've come to town."

Quickly Charles scanned the note and looked up. A short distance away, Teddy stood shifting uneasily from foot to foot, a doomed expression on his face. When Charles crooked his finger he came. Not readily, but he came.

"Good evening, Lady Cromley." He bowed deeply, then faced Charles. "Yes, Chas?"

"Explain this," he said, showing him the letter.

"I can't," Teddy admitted, "other than to tell you I had a brilliant plan in my head at the time. Unfortunately I can't remember what it was."

"I had no idea," Lady Cromley said, with a laugh, "that forgetfulness runs in the family."

"So do hot tempers and a tendency to throttle meddlers," Charles growled.

"Then before you quiz her on it," Teddy went on hurriedly, "let me confess I never heard Lady Cromley say anything. I only heard what Lesley said and repeated it."

"To what purpose?"

"To pry you away from your books, Chas. You were becoming as musty as an old tome."

"At least that's the truth."

"Well, of course it's the truth. Why would I lie?" When Charles arched a brow at him he flushed. "Touché. But I give you my word I've no other schemes in the works."

"For the moment at least," Charles replied, slipping a hand beneath Lady Cromley's elbow. "While we dance this waltz, I expect you to correct the misconstruction Lady Betsy has made."

"I tried, Chas, I truly did," Teddy said earnestly. "But she wouldn't believe me."

"Fancy that," Charles observed dryly.

"Oh, dear," Lady Cromley said worriedly. "Not that old drivel again?"

"Not to worry, Caro. Teddy will see to it." He paused and gave his brother a humorless smile. "Won't you, Teddy?"

"This instant."

Wheeling away, he hurried after Betsy, who was settling her grandmother in a chair among the other chaperones. Once Teddy reached her side, Charles led Lady Cromley onto the floor.

"I had no idea my presence would cause a problem," she said.

"Think nothing of it, Caro. It's a pleasure to see you, as always," he replied, leading her into the dance, but watching over the top of her head as Betsy rounded on Teddy and jabbed a finger into his cravat.

"She is very lovely."

Charles dragged his gaze away from Betsy and saw Lady Cromley smiling at him knowingly.

"Her name is Elizabeth Keaton," he told her. "She's kindness itself, capricious as the wind, amazingly intelligent, silly as a goose, and utterly infuriating."

"And you are madly in love with her."

"Yes, God help me."

"I couldn't be happier for you, though I can't say love becomes you." Lady Cromley smiled, her eyes shining with amusement. "You look an absolute wreck."

"Would you believe that since I've met her I've been knocked senseless twice by her dog, had a sleeve torn out of my coat, been hit in the jaw with her reticule, threatened with a dagger, and bashed over the head with a copy of Ovid's *Amores*?"

"How utterly famous." Lady Cromley laughed gaily. "She's *perfect* for you, Charles."

"Yes, I know." He grinned at her.

One of the violins—or was it one of the horns— hit a sour note just then. At least that's what Charles thought it was until he heard it again.

"Someone did not tune their instrument properly," Lady Cromley remarked, glancing at the orchestra set up on a dais in one of the far corners.

"I don't think so. I've never heard anything like it, but I don't believe—"

And Charles couldn't a moment later, when Boru came bursting through one of the French windows. Sliding on the slippery floor, he sat back on his haunches, threw back his great head, and loosed a mournful howl that drew screams from the women and brought the orchestra to a screeching, bleating halt.

"Good heavens!" Lady Cromley gasped. "What *is* that?"

"*Boru!*" Betsy cried joyfully, her voice ringing across the ballroom. "Boru! Here, boy!"

Scrambling up on all fours, the hound flung his head around. When he saw Betsy, he gave a deep, throaty bark and launched himself straight across the dance floor with kite strings still trailing from his coat. Couples scrambled to remove themselves from his path, skirts billowed, gentlemen spun in circles, and shrieks rang. As Boru galloped past, slipping and sliding, his nails unable to find a purchase on the marble floor, Charles foresaw disaster as Betsy had foreseen it the day before in Hyde Park.

"Excuse me, Caro," he said, breaking into a run to intercept the hound.

The footing was no better for him than it was for Boru. Or for Betsy and Teddy rushing toward him from the opposite direction. Marble floors were simply not made for running. Projecting Boru's course, Charles realized the punch table and Lady Featherston lay directly in his path to Betsy. The countess, an ample matron in a plum-colored gown, stood rooted to the spot with a cup of punch half raised, her mouth agape at the huge, shaggy creature pelting toward her.

"My lady, move!" Charles shouted at her.

She did, slamming her cup down and hiking her skirts to flee, but too late. The last-second course correction Boru attempted failed and he went crashing into the punch table. The leg he collided with snapped in two and stacks of crystal cups toppled. The punch bowl rolled heavily on its side and spewed its contents all over Lady Featherston.

The shriek the countess gave silenced all the others. No one dared to even twitter at the sight of her, dripping with punch and quivering with fury. The guests held their breath—as did Charles—waiting to see what she would do, which was nothing but quiver and drip until Betsy went down on her knees to embrace Boru. Then the countess spun toward her, flicking drops of punch from her fingertips.

"Is that beast yours?" she demanded.

Slowly Betsy rose to her feet, her face pale but her chin lifted. "Yes, my lady," she replied, catching Boru's collar firmly in her hand.

Lady Featherston said nothing else, simply turned her back on Betsy. A second matron followed suit, then a third, along with her portly escort.

The cut direct.

Betsy felt her heart plummet to her toes and a wave of hot shame flood her face. A fourth couple and then a fifth turned their backs on her, but she lifted her chin higher and bit back tears. When Teddy stepped boldly up beside her, she shot him a panicked glance.

"Turn away from me this instant."

"I won't," he said, glaring defiantly about the ballroom. "And neither will Charles."

"Oh, no," Betsy moaned, turning away from Teddy to see Charles striding purposefully toward her, pushing his way, and none too gently, through the about-faced crowd.

Through his peephole in the palms, Julian saw him, too, but couldn't believe it. Braxton should not be moving to intervene, he should be cutting Betsy direct with the rest of the ton. It was the hinge pin of his plan. What in blazes was wrong with the man? Didn't he realize, didn't he care, that he, too, would be a social outcast?

In point of fact, Charles did not. He cared only for Betsy and the undeserved humiliation being heaped upon her. That stopping before her and offering his hand was the perfect way to redeem himself with her never occurred to him.

"My lady," he said. "I believe this is our waltz."

A gasp or two sounded in the crowd close by, but Charles ignored them. Teddy grinned, closed his hand over Boru's collar, and gave Betsy a nudge in the ribs with his elbow.

She shot him a glare, then looked squarely at Charles. "You needn't do this, Your Grace. I don't care a fig for any of these people."

But she did, for Charles could see it in the paleness of her face and the quiver of her lips.

"Neither do I, but I do care for you, dearest Betsy. Far more than is prudent, which is the reason I keep making a fool of myself, I'm sure." Charles smiled and offered his hand again. "Now waltz with me, my darling."

"Oh, *Charles*," Betsy breathed, hardly able to believe what she was hearing.

"At last, you say my name." He grinned, tucked her hand in the curve of his arm, and led her onto the dance floor.

With a sharp look aimed at the orchestra, the music began again as quickly as it had stopped. A tear spilled from Betsy's right eye, but Charles brushed it away with his thumb and took her into his arms. They danced the first three bars alone, then Teddy swung Lady Cromley onto the floor. Boru, Charles saw over Betsy's head, was safely in the grasp of Lady Clymore.

When another couple joined them, then two more and four more, Betsy lifted her face to Charles and smiled. Tremulously, with tears still gleaming in her eyes.

"You see, darling," he said to her, "sometimes it pays to be a duke and have the power to order people about."

"Yes, I see that now," Betsy agreed, her eyes shining with relief and mischief, "and am ever so glad, after all, that you are a tyrant."

Charles laughed, pulled her closer, and murmured in her ear, "You will marry me, won't you, Betsy darling?"

"I suppose I shall have to," she replied, drawing back and feigning a weary sigh, "if for no other reason than to keep you from making a fool of yourself at every turn."

"Is that the only reason?"

"Well, no, I—" Betsy paused, glanced around at the now-crowded floor, then lifted a radiant smile to Charles and murmured softly, "I love you with all my heart."

With the final strains of the waltz came a clatter outside the French windows. A thud, a howl, and a crash followed, then George appeared in the doorway with Davey and a smallish man in a many-caped greatcoat clenched in his beefy hand.

The sight of the footman in muddied livery and the boy in a torn velvet jacket altered for him from one of Betsy's riding habits was too much for the Countess Featherston. She fainted dead away near the punch table, while the rest of her guests separated into small groups twittering with speculation.

"Enter the jarvey, I'll wager," Charles said, taking Betsy by the hand and leading her hurriedly toward George.

"Got 'im, m'lord," George said, grasping his captive by the scruff of the neck and hauling him up on his feet to face Charles. "Caught 'im in the garden lettin' Boru loose and chasin' 'im toward the house."

"Who hired you to do this?"

"I ain't sayin' nothin'," Owens snarled.

"Wanna bet?" Davey piped in, coming around George to kick the jarvey squarely in the shins.

"Ow!" he howled, bending to rub his leg.

"Davey, come here." A grin tugging the corners of her mouth, Betsy caught the boy by the sleeve and tried her best to look stern as she dragged him out of the way.

Then she signed to Teddy, who nodded and moved to reclaim Boru from Lady Clymore. He led the hound toward them, and when Boru saw the jarvey, he laid back his ears and began to growl.

"On second thought," Owens said quickly, "it was that there Earl o' Clymore paid me t'do it."

"Owens, you idiot!" Julian screeched, unthinkingly stepping out of his hiding place.

At the sight of him, Boru let out a howl and lunged, breaking Teddy's hold on his collar. Lord Earnshaw went sprawling on his face, and Julian went tearing through the French windows with the hound on his heels.

"Get him, Boru!" Betsy yelled, grasping Davey's hand as Charles grabbed hers and pulled her into a run.

Like a stag in flight, Julian vaulted the low wall enclosing the terrace. Boru sailed effortlessly after him, while Charles and Betsy and Davey prudently took the steps. By the time they reached the lawn, Teddy had caught up with them, and Boru had narrowed the gap with Julian by several yards.

The upstart had two choices—a sturdy oak or the far wall enclosing the garden. Charles thought he would opt for a low-hanging branch of the tree, and that's precisely what he did, jumping to catch it and swing himself up into the first crotch. Beneath him, Boru let out another howl and leapt up the trunk, snarling and yapping.

"The fox is caught," Teddy said, with a laugh, as they slowed their pace from a run to a leisurely walk.

By the time they reached the foot of the tree, Julian had scrambled higher, and Boru had sat patiently down on his haunches to wait. The Earl of Clymore glared balefully down at them, his face glimmering with perspiration in the glow of the lanterns strung about the lawn.

"Call him off," he snarled at Betsy.

"Oh, I will, Julian," she replied sweetly, "just as soon as I'm ready to go home."

"*What?*" he squawked. "That could be hours!"

"I'm sure it *will* be, for I intend to dance every

dance." Betsy slid her hand through Charles's arm and smiled. "With my fiancé."

"Bit chilly up there, is it, Clymore?" Charles peered up at him and grinned.

"Damn your eyes, Braxton," Julian growled, his teeth beginning to chatter.

"Better get used to it," Charles advised. "Newgate is cold as hell. So is France, I'm told."

"Elizabeth, *please*," Julian begged, shifting his attention to his cousin. "Don't leave me here."

"I'm afraid it's not up to me," she said, patting Boru on his broad, shaggy head. "What do you think, my darling? Should we let him down?"

Boru rumbled and growled and inched closer to the tree.

"Sorry, Julian. Boru says no." Betsy gave him a jaunty wave, then turned toward the house with Charles.

"Up you go, lad," Teddy said to Davey, lifting the boy onto his shoulders and striding ahead of them.

When Julian's howls of protest and pleading fell away into the darkness behind them, Charles turned Betsy toward him and slipped his arms gently about her waist. She spread her palms on his chest and smiled at him, her hair dancing with tiny diamonds of light in the sheen of the lanterns.

"I have only one request of you, my darling," he murmured, drawing her closer to kiss her.

"For you, my lord, anything." She sighed dreamily. "What is it?"

"Let's leave Boru at home on our wedding trip."